LACERATIONS

K.G. LEWIS

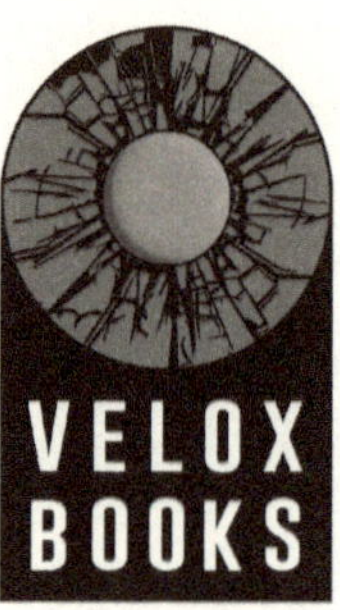

VELOX
BOOKS

YOU'RE READING ANOTHER TERRIFYING COLLECTION FROM

FOLLOW VELOX TO KEEP THE NIGHTMARES COMING:

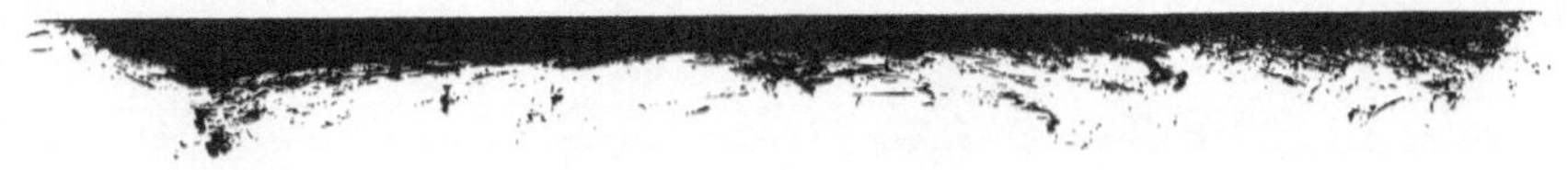

This book is dedicated to Elizabeth for always being there when I needed feedback.

CONTENTS

PARANORMAL PEST CONTROL

I knocked on the door of the modest single-story home.

When nobody answered, I knocked again, louder, and called out "Pest Control," announcing who I was.

A moment later, the door creaked open.

"Hi, I'm...," I didn't get the rest of the words out of my mouth because I was stunned at the appearance of the woman who had opened the door.

Quickly regaining my composure, I succeeded in introducing myself.

"Hi, I'm Nate from Paranormal Pest Control." I tapped the name patch that was sewn onto my uniform, "I'm guessing this is why you called." I gestured at the thick layer of spiderwebs that covered the woman's entire body.

She nodded, "I don't know where they came from," her voice was muffled due to the webbing covering her mouth, "And no matter how hard I try," she reached up and pulled at the webs around her face, "I can't get rid of them." As soon as she let go, the webs fused together, hiding her face again.

"Do you mind if I come in and take a look around, see if I can locate the source of these uncanny webs?"

"Of course not," she stepped aside to let me enter the home.

I spent the next 30 minutes searching every room in her house, including the attic, but I couldn't find any bugs in the place, not even an ant. The place was spotless.

"Any luck?" she asked when I caught up with her in the kitchen.

"Not yet," I shook my head, "But there's still one more place I need to check." I walked over to the door to let myself out.

"Where're you going?"

"Outside to check the crawlspace under the house."

After retrieving my flashlight from the truck, I squeezed through the little access gate that led under the house and began searching the confined area for signs of what was causing the webs on the woman.

I didn't find what I was looking for until I made my way over to the opposite side of the crawlspace, where I found a patch of dirt that was higher than the surrounding area indicating something was buried there.

"Bingo," I declared, shining my light at the spot.

I was certain I had found what I was looking for and set about digging it up.

Once I got it free, I carried it to the front of the house to show the woman what it was.

"Is that a body?" she gasped after I'd laid the web-shrouded bundle of bones onto the porch

"It is," I confirmed.

"Whose?"

"Yours."

I pulled the webs off the bones, revealing the tattered clothing underneath. As soon as I did that, the webs that were wrapped around the woman's body started disappearing, revealing that she was wearing the same clothing as the skeleton.

She began sobbing in disbelief.

"Is there someone I can call?" I asked, "Someone who might be looking for you?"

Before the woman could reply, she faded from view.

MOMMY DEAREST

"Where's the rest of the money?!" Chad yelled into the old lady's face.

We'd broken into her home after hearing from a fellow convict we served time with that she had $10,000 hidden somewhere in the house.

"That's all I have," she whimpered, gesturing at the meager collection of bills and coins Chad had pulled out of her purse and tossed onto the kitchen table.

"Stop lying." Chad pressed his gun against the lady's temple, "We know you've got more hidden somewhere. Tell us where it is and you won't get hurt."

The old lady turned and looked at me. She was terrified. I could see it written all over her face. I even thought I caught a whiff of urine, making me think she had pissed her pants.

"Maybe she doesn't have it," I suggested to Chad.

If she was as scared as she looked, I was certain she would have given us money if she had it.

"I'm not leaving here without the money." He swung the gun in my direction, "Search the place." He gestured with the pistol. "If she won't tell us where it is, we'll just have to find it ourselves."

I knew better than to protest when Chad was like that, so I started searching the kitchen, looking for something I knew we'd never find. While I did that, Chad walked into the adjoining living room and began searching there.

"Please be careful with that," the old lady begged.

I turned and saw Chad holding an antique porcelain doll in his hand.

"It was my daughter's," she explained.

"Sounds like the perfect place to hide some cash," Chad said, raising the doll over his head before slamming it down onto a nearby coffee table.

When the doll broke, it shattered into a hundred pieces and expelled a massive cloud of fine grey dust.

"You shouldn't have done that," the old lady said.

"What the fuck was in that thing?" Chad coughed as he yelled before brushing the dust from his clothes.

"My daughter's ashes," she replied.

"I should shoot you right now," Chad snarled.

When he finished speaking, I felt the room grow cold. Cold enough that I could see my breath. A moment later, all of the cabinets and drawers began to rattle.

After a while, it felt like the whole house was shaking.

"What's going on?" I looked over at the lady.

"I told him to be careful," she said to me.

"We should go," I called out, but my words were cut off when the door between the rooms slammed shut.

"Where the fuck did you come from?" I heard Chad's muffled voice through the door.

There shouldn't have been anyone in the room with him.

"I live here," a young girl replied to Chad's question, "Where the fuck did you come from?"

There was a brief moment of silence.

"Get away from me!" Chad suddenly yelled. "I mean it." His threat was followed by a gunshot.

The girl giggled. Chad screamed.

GOLD DIGGER

“I appreciate you coming to see me at this late hour, Mr. Flynn,” the lawyer said as I entered his office. “Please have a seat,” he gestured at the chair in front of his desk.

“It’s no trouble,” I said, taking the offered seat.

“As you know,” the lawyer continued, “Your late wife appointed me the executor of her will,” he adjusted some papers on his desk, “One of the things she requested is that you and I meet alone to go over it before I read it to the rest of the family.”

Finally, I thought, *all those years of being married to that wrinkled old fart were going to pay off.*

Most people knew I’d married her for the money, but she didn’t care about that because I made her feel young again.

“What did she leave me?”

I’d already had to wait a week to see the lawyer. I couldn’t bear to wait any longer. I desperately wanted to know what she’d left me in her will.

“We’ll get to that,” the lawyer pushed himself up from the desk, “First, we’re going to have a drink.”

The lawyer walked over to the liquor cabinet in the corner of his office and poured himself a glass of bourbon.

"What'll you have?" he gestured at the bottles arranged in the cabinet.

"Whatever you're having is fine with me," I replied, wanting him to hurry up and sit back down so we could get on with it.

The lawyer poured my drink and then carried it over to me.

"To Alice," he held his drink out in a toast to my dead wife.

"To Alice," I repeated, clinking my glass against his.

He took a sip of his while I downed mine in one gulp.

"Can we get back to it now?" I asked.

"Of course," he replied, walking back around the desk to take his seat, "Would you like a copy of the will?" he lifted a piece of paper off the desk and held it out to me.

"Sure," the word sounded weird coming out of my mouth. Like I'd said it in slow-motion.

I tried to reach out to take the paper from him, but I couldn't get my arm to move.

"Wha...," I was trying to say *What's going on* but found I couldn't get my mouth to form the words.

A moment later, my head fell forward onto the lawyer's desk as I passed out.

"What the fuck is going on?" I hissed.

When I regained consciousness, I found myself lying on the ground next to my wife's grave with my arms and legs bound. Standing above me was the lawyer.

"As per the terms laid out in your wife's will," the lawyer said, "You're to be buried alongside her."

When he was done speaking, he kicked me into the hole where I landed on top of my wife's casket.

A moment later, a steady stream of dirt began raining down upon me.

THE TEXT

Andre was waiting for me near the top of the stairwell so we could walk to fourth period together.

He looked upset about something, prompting me to ask, "What's up?"

"You haven't gotten any strange texts, have you?" he asked.

"No," I replied. "Why?"

Andre pulled out his phone and showed me the screen. On it was a text from an unknown sender that read:

Wh_ weren't y_u at my f_neral service? Th_t was _eally rud_. It's o_ly b_en si_ days and already you have forgo_ten me.

"That's creepy," I said, "When'd you get it?"

"Right before you walked up." He started to put his phone away, but I stopped him.

"Hold up." I motioned for him to give it to me. "Let me see it for a second."

"Why?"

"I want to see something."

When I read the text, I noticed the missing letters but didn't think anything of them. Now that I had a moment to think, I wanted to take a closer look at them.

He slapped the phone into my outstretched palm.

I reread the text, this time taking note of every letter that was missing.

"You are next," I declared, handing the phone back to him.

"What?" He looked confused.

"The missing letters," I explained, "That's what they spell out. You. Are. Next."

Andre looked down at his phone to confirm what I had told him.

"It's probably one of Cassie's friends fucking with you for not going to the funeral," I suggested.

Cassie was a classmate who died after a party a month ago. She lost control of her car and drove into the lake.

There was a rumor going around that she and Andre had hooked up at the party a few hours before she died. I never asked him about it because it seemed in poor taste to be talking about Cassie like that.

"You're probably right," he agreed, putting his phone away, "Let's get to class before..." He stopped speaking to stare at something over my shoulder. "Do you see that?" he pointed.

"See what?" I turned but didn't see anything.

Whatever he was seeing terrified him. He took a step back and then another, unaware of how close he was to the stairs.

"WATCH OUT!" I tried to grab him, but I was too far away. All I could do was watch as Andre fell backward down the stairs.

The official police report listed Andre's death as an accident, but I knew it wasn't an accident. Right before he fell, I felt a cold chill pass through my body. With that chill came a vision of what happened to Cassie that night and the part Andre played in her death.

I also learned that Andre wasn't the only one responsible. Cassie had a list of people she blamed. Andre was just the beginning of her vengeance.

The night Andre died, I received the same text he did, but only three letters were missing from mine, an S and two H's.

FAIRYTALE ENDING

"This looks like the right place," the knight said, rolling up the map and shoving it back into its case before climbing out of the saddle.

His horse neighed, vocalizing the unease it felt, "This place creeps me out too," he patted the animal's neck, "But we've got a job to do. One that will make us rich, so that we'll never have to travel this far from home again. Doesn't that sound nice?"

The knight turned and approached the ancient tower, surprised to see that its thick wooden door was slightly ajar. He was told that it would be locked.

"Hello?" he called out, drawing his sword and using the tip to push the door the rest of the way open.

The creaking of its old iron hinges is the only response he got.

He stepped through the doorway and into the interior of the tower. As soon as he crossed the threshold, the door slammed shut behind him. He tried to open it, but it wouldn't budge.

"What kind of sorcery is this?" the knight muttered.

In the corner of the large circular room, something began to clatter in the shadows.

That must be the tower's guardian, the knight thought.

He readied his sword and took a battle stance, waiting for whatever it was to show itself.

When the first skeleton appeared, clattering its way towards him, he smiled.

A skeleton, that's it? I was expecting something a bit more challenging.

He raised his sword, preparing to strike the undead creature, but stopped when he saw the second and then the third skeleton.

How many of them are there?

The answer to his question was more than he could count.

Realizing he would be overwhelmed if he stayed where he was, he ran up the stairs and didn't stop until he reached the door at the top.

The knight threw the door open and slammed it shut behind him. It only took him a moment to realize he wasn't alone.

Standing across the room from him was the most beautiful maiden he had ever seen.

"Princess," he bowed, "I am Sir Alder, a knight in your father's kingdom. I've been sent to rescue you."

"Come closer so that I may see you better," she beckoned.

Sir Alder obliged, taking two quick strides across the room, but he didn't get to take a third as the floor suddenly disappeared beneath him.

He had fallen through a trap door that was covered by a flimsy rug. It sent him plummeting from the top of the tower, all the way to the bottom where he landed on a pile of skeletons. The same skeletons that had threatened him earlier, but they were no longer animated.

As he lay there, the princess appeared by his side, "If you survive, you can tell my father he's too late. If not, you can join the other guardians," she gestured at the pile of bones.

When she finished delivering her message, she faded from view.

SHOW AND TELL

"Thank you for sharing your grandfather's medals with us, Tyler," Ms. Morton said. "The story about how he got them was incredible. Does anyone have any questions for Tyler?"

Nobody responded.

"Go ahead and take your seat," she gave Tyler a gentle push on the back.

Tyler put his grandfather's medals back in their display case and then returned to his seat.

"Alright, Erica, it looks like you're next," Ms. Morton gestured for her to come to the front of the class.

Erica picked up the ornate wooden box that had been sitting on her desk and walked to the front of the class.

"That's a pretty box," Ms. Morton said, "Did someone in your family make that?"

Erica nodded, "My grandpa carved it out of Rowan wood. He said he used Rowan wood because it has a lot of magical properties."

A couple of the kids in the class snickered at the idea of the wood having magical properties.

"That's enough," Ms. Morton said to the class. To Erica she said, "What kind of magical properties?"

"Erica shrugged, "I don't know, I never asked him."

"Well, it truly is a lovely box," Ms. Morton said in a tone suggesting that Erica's show-and-tell presentation was over.

"The box isn't what I wanted to show everyone," Erica said, looking up at Ms. Morton, "I want to show them what's inside."

"Oh, ok," Ms. Morton placed a hand on Erica's shoulder, "I'm sorry, go ahead and show the class what you brought for show and tell."

Erica set the box on the corner of Ms. Morton's desk, slowly lifted the lid, and then reached inside to pull out a small, handmade doll.

"What's that?" Ms. Morton asked, the look on her face showing her disgust for the crudely made doll.

"This is a voodoo doll," Erica said, proudly holding the doll up so everyone in the class could see it, "My grandma helped me make it. She said she's been making them since she was my age. She has hundreds of them in her bedroom."

"I don't think…" Ms. Morton was trying to tell Erica that she didn't think the voodoo doll was an appropriate show-and-tell item, but she couldn't speak. No matter how hard she tried, she couldn't force the words out.

"This voodoo doll is of Ms. Morton," Erica told the class, "As long as I keep my hand over her mouth like this, she can't speak."

To prove her point, she removed her hand. As soon as she did, Ms. Morton cried out.

"Erica!" she yelled, but that was the only word she got out before Erica placed her hand back over the doll's mouth.

Still able to move, Ms. Morton tried to take the doll away from Erica, but she was too slow.

In response, Erica grabbed the doll's legs and started twisting them. Not enough to break them, just enough to cause Ms. Morton a great deal of pain.

"Sit down," Erica said.

Ms. Morton quickly obeyed.

GRANDMA

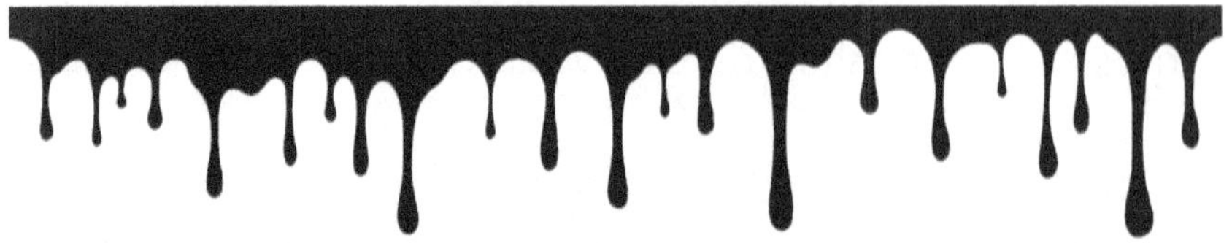

His mom placed her hand on his back and looked down at him. "Are you ready, Casey?" she asked.

Casey looked up at her and nodded. "I'm ready." The tone of his voice implied the opposite.

"Are you sure?" she asked. "You don't have to do this if you don't want to."

"I'm sure," he replied.

His mom reached down and took his hand, giving it a gentle squeeze before leading him into the funeral parlor where his grandmother's casket sat on a catafalque surrounded by flowers.

"If you change your mind, let me know," she said as they took their place at the end of the line, "I won't be upset."

"I want to do it," Casey insisted and then added, "I have to do it."

"No you don't," his mom shook her head.

Yes, I do, he thought to himself.

"She's going to look like she's sleeping," his mom explained as the line moved up, "But she's not. She's gone."

The way his mom was going on about his grandmother made Casey think that she was more nervous about being there than he was.

"I know she's not sleeping, Mom" he said, sounding a little more annoyed than he intended.

She squeezed his hand again, "I know you do."

Neither of them spoke again until it was almost their turn to view the casket.

"We're next," his mom said.

Casey reached into the pocket of his jacket and wrapped his hand around the object he'd brought with him.

"Alright," she said as the couple in front of them walked away, "It's our turn."

She released Casey's hand so she could reach into her purse and pull out a tissue as they approached the casket.

"Goodbye, mom," she said, her voice catching in her throat as she spoke.

Casey looked up at her and saw that she was crying.

"Is there anything you want to say to her?" his mom asked as she used the tissue to wipe away the tears.

Casey nodded.

"Goodbye, grandma," he said, pulling the object out of his pocket and dropping it into the casket.

"What was that?" his mom asked, leaning over the casket to see what Casey had dropped inside of it.

"It's a compass," Casey replied.

"The one I just bought you?"

He nodded.

Casey had asked his mom to buy him the compass the day before the funeral. She'd originally tried to buy him a toy one, but he insisted on getting a real one, which wasn't cheap.

"Why did you put the compass in her casket?" she couldn't understand why he'd want to give it away.

"It's to help grandma find her way to heaven," Casey said.

"Oh, honey," she gave him a weak smile and started to cry again, "She doesn't need help finding her way to heaven. She's already there."

Casey looked at his mom with a confused look on his face, "If she's already in Heaven, why do I keep seeing her at our house?"

DEATH WALKS INTO A BAR

Everyone stopped what they were doing when the skeletal figure in the black robe stepped through the entrance of the pub. In his left hand was a scythe which he held like a walking stick.

It was clear who he was.

Death looked around the now quiet room before proceeding to the bar.

All eyes followed him as he slowly made his way up to the bar, tapping the handle of his scythe on the floor as he walked.

The bartender had to force himself to greet the ancient being.

"H-h-how can I h-h-help you?" he stuttered, unable to keep his fear from affecting his voice.

"I am looking for a particular man," Death said, his voice was deep and hollow and seemed to echo within his skull. "He goes by the name of Bob Smith. Do you know him?"

"N-n-no, I d-d-don't," the bartender replied. "Perhaps you've g-g-got the wrong b-b-bar." Even though he was relieved Death wasn't looking for him, he was still intimidated by his presence.

"This is the Soggy Rose, is it not?" Death asked, turning to look around the room again.

"It is," the bartender confirmed.

"Then this is the right bar." Death returned his attention to the bartender. "Perhaps one of your patrons can point the man out."

"Yeah, m-m-maybe," the bartender agreed. "I'll ask them."

"I appreciate it," Death turned around and leaned against the bar to wait.

"Hey!" the bartender yelled to make sure everyone could hear him,

"Does anyone here know a B-B-Bob Smith?"

Most of the people in the bar looked around at their friends and neighbors before shaking their heads.

A moment later, a man sitting at one of the tables stood up and pointed across the bar at another man who was sitting in a corner booth by himself. The man was hunkered down as if he were trying to hide.

"If I had to guess," the man who stood up said, "I'd say that was Bob Smith."

There were several murmurs of agreement.

Death walked across the room and stopped in front of the man's table.

"Is that true?" Death asked, "Are you Bob Smith?"

Bob Smith considered lying for a moment, but then thought better of it. If Death had come looking for him, lying about who he was wouldn't change things, he'd catch up to him sooner or later.

"Yes," Bob replied as he sat up straighter in the booth, "I'm Bob Smith."

If I'm going to die, he thought to himself, *I'm at least going to die with a little dignity.*

"Stand up," Death said.

"Can I finish my drink first?" he asked meekly.

"Stand. Up." Death emphasized each word.

"Okay, okay" Bob slid out of the booth and quickly got to his feet, "I'm up."

"I need you to leave," Death pointed towards the exit with his scythe.

"Excuse me?" Bob asked, thinking he hadn't heard Death correctly.

"I said leave," Death repeated, "You're not a part of what's about to happen here."

CAT'S EYE

"Here you go," Jackson said, handing the TV remote to Holly, "Why don't you find us something to watch while I go to the kithen and make us some popcorn."

"Okay," she smiled, "I hope you like horror movies," she aimed the remote at the television and selected horror from the list of categories.

Jackson and Holly had only been dating for a couple of weeks, and this was the first time that Jackson had invited Holly back to his apartment.

While Jackson was in the kitchen, Holly started scrolling through horror movies on the streaming app, trying to find something that she hadn't already seen. That was when she saw the black and orange tortoiseshell cat walk out of the hallway.

"Hey, kitty, kitty," she said softly to the cat, reaching out her hand, trying to get it to walk closer so she could pet it.

The cat ignored her, choosing to walk over to the corner of the room and started grooming itself instead.

"Typical tortie," Holly muttered.

As she watched the cat, its ears suddenly perked up, and it began to stare at a spot in the corner of the room about five feet off of the ground.

Holly tried to see what the cat was looking but she couldn't see anything from where she was sitting. Thinking that the cat might have found a bug, she got up and took a few steps toward the corner of the room.

"What the heck are you looking at?" she asked the cat, still not seeing anything.

The cat turned its head to briefly meow at her before returning its attention to the spot on the wall.

"You're starting to creep me out," she said, suddenly getting a chill.

The cat suddenly stood up, arched its back, and started hissing.

"What're you doing?" Jackson asked, walking back into the living room to find that Holly wasn't sitting on the couch any longer. In his hands was a big bowl of popcorn.

"Jesus Christ!" she jumped and whirled around to face him, "You just scared the shit out of me."

"Sorry," he apologized, "I didn't mean to."

"Do you believe in ghosts?" Holly asked.

"Ghosts?" Jackson repeated, caught off guard by the unexpected question.

"Yeah, ghosts, haunted houses, that sort of thing," she said.

"Why do you ask?" Since he really liked Holly, he didn't want to give a wrong answer, so he was stalling, trying to get her to give her opinion on the matter first.

"I ask because I think your cat might be staring at one right now," she pointed at the corner of the room.

Jackson looked at where Holly was pointing before turning to look at her with a confused look on his face. "What cat?" he asked, seeing nothing there. "I don't have a cat."

HOUSE HUNTING

"Do you have any kids?" the realtor asked.

"I do," I replied, "A son."

"How old?"

"Five," I said, "Almost six."

"Is he in kindergarten yet?"

"Not yet. He starts this fall, which is why I'm out here looking at houses."

I currently live in a small two-bedroom apartment on the opposite side of town. The area most residents referred to as the bad side of town.

I'd recently gotten promoted to a management position and decided it was time to move. The increase in salary I received would finally allow me to afford a place of my own. One where I could lay down roots for my son's future.

"The schools in this area are phenomenal," the realtor said.

I already knew that. I'd done my research before I called the realtor.

"So, what do you think of the place so far?" the realtor was standing in the middle of the living room, holding her arms out.

"I like it a lot better than the other ones you showed me," I replied. "The floorplan is more open, it has a fenced-in backyard, and it is a little bit closer to work for me."

"I thought you might like this one best," the realtor smiled, "That's why I saved it for last." She started walking towards the hall, "Wait until you see the bedrooms."

The realtor showed me the first two bedrooms in the house. Both were pretty standard looking, one faced the front of the house, and the other faced the backyard.

"I think my son would like this one," I remarked about the room facing the backyard. It was the bigger of the two.

"The current owners are looking to sell quickly," the realtor said as we walked down the hall to the master bedroom. "If you put in a reasonable offer, I'm certain they'd accept it."

"I'll keep that in mind," I said, following the realtor into the master bedroom and looking around.

"Nice, right?" the realtor gestured at the room around us.

I didn't answer. I was overcome by a sudden feeling of déjà vu. "I've seen this room before," I declared.

"Really?" the realtor didn't know what else to say.

"Yeah," I said, "But I can't..." I was about to say I couldn't remember where when it suddenly hit me where I saw it.

I reached into my purse and pulled out the drawing my son had given me before I dropped him off at the babysitter's house.

I unfolded it and compared it to the room I was in. The drawing matched exactly.

I showed the drawing to the realtor.

"Your son drew this?" she asked.

I nodded, "I'd forgotten about it until just now."

"Who's that supposed to be?" the realtor pointed at the shadowy figure my son had drawn peeking out from behind the curtains. The curtain I was currently standing next to.

"I hadn't noticed that before," I said.

"Your son is quite the artist," something whispered in my ear.

TICK TOCK

"When did that get here?" I stopped and muttered.

I'd just clocked out from my shift at the record shop and was walking to the exit when I saw that the mall had a new shop.

"Tick Tock Clock Shop," I read the shop's name from the lighted sign above the entryway.

I'd only been off for a day and was surprised to see how fast it had moved in. Two days ago, the space was empty.

Curious, I decided to pop inside and see what kind of person worked in a clock shop.

If I'm lucky, he'll be cute and smart, and won't be interested in Tabitha.

Tabitha was my manager at the record shop and there wasn't a single guy working at the mall that she hadn't slept with. That is of course an exaggeration, but it certainly felt that way to me.

"Welcome to Tick Tock Clock Shop," the elderly man behind the counter greeted me with a smile.

I couldn't hide my disappointment at seeing him instead of someone closer to my own age.

"So," I looked around the shop, seeing nothing but a wide variety of clocks, both antique and modern. The place looked like a museum detailing the history of timekeeping. "You sell clocks?"

I felt like an idiot as soon as the comment was out of my mouth.

Way to go captain obvious, I chided herself, wishing I had just left the mall like I had intended.

"Actually," the old man replied, "None of these clocks are for sale." He swept his hand across the shop, "They are display pieces. I use them to advertise the invaluable service I'm offering here."

"And what service is it that you offer?"

"Time," the old man said.

"Time?"

He nodded.

"Take a closer look at one of those clocks," he insisted, gesturing at the timepieces that were nearest to me.

I rolled my eyes and looked at the nearest clock.

That's weird.

I immediately noticed that it wasn't displaying the correct time. Stranger yet, it was counting backward.

"I think your clocks are broken," I said.

"I assure you, they are working fine," he replied.

"Then why are they counting backwards?"

"They're showing you how much time you have left to live," the old man explained, "And from the look of it, you haven't got much left."

If what he was saying was true, I was supposed to die in just over four hours.

"I don't believe you," I said.

"I'm not here to convince you," he replied, "I'm just here to offer you more time if you want it."

"Whatever," I scoffed, "I am not falling for whatever scam you've got going on here." I turned and started walking out of the store.

"This is a one-time offer," the old man called out as I left, "Once you leave, you won't get a second chance."

"That's fine by me," I whirled around to yell at him, but there was nothing there but an empty shop.

HAWKEYE

"What's this?" Own asked, pulling open the large cardboard box that was sitting on the table.

"Just some old junk of mine from when I was a kid," his dad replied, "Your grandfather found it when he was cleaning out the attic."

"What arc you going to do with it?"

He walked over and put a hand on Owen's shoulder. "I was going to see if you wanted any of it before I gave it to the thrift store."

"Really?" Owen looked up at him.

"Really," his dad insisted with a smile.

Owen grabbed the box with two hands and dragged it off the table, struggling to keep it in his arms.

It's heavier than it looks, he thought.

"Need some help with that?" his dad asked.

"Nope," Owen grunted, determined to carry it on his own. "I got it."

His dad smiled as he watched me carry the box of old toys down the hall to his room.

———————

Owen's mom walked into the living room. "It's kind of late for Owen to be having a friend over, don't you think?" she said.

"I don't remember anyone coming to the door," Owen's dad replied.

It had been a couple of hours since Owen had taken the box of toys back to his room. During that time, his dad was in the living room watching a football game on the television.

"Well, he's back there talking to someone," she jerked her thumb over her shoulder toward the hallway.

"I'll go see what's up."

He pushed himself up from the recliner and walked down the hall, stopping when he got to Owen's room.

Just like his wife had said, he could hear his son talking to someone.

"Knock, knock," he said, tapping his knuckles against the door as he spoke.

"Come in," Owen called out.

His dad opened the door and peeked his head inside. "Who are you...," he stopped speaking when he didn't see anyone else but Owen in the room.

"Are you alone in here?" he asked.

"Yeah, why?"

"I would've sworn I just heard you talking to someone."

"I was," Owen admitted, "With this." He lifted an old boxy-looking walkie-talkie that was lying on the bed next to him. "I found it in the box you gave me. Watch."

Owen lifted the walkie-talkie to his mouth and pressed the button on the side of it.

"Owen to Hawkeye. Come in Hawkeye," he said into the microphone.

"Hawkeye here," came the staticky response.

"My dad wanted to know who I was talking to," Owen said into the walkie-talkie.

"Give me that," his dad said, snatching the walkie-talkie out of Owen's hand. He turned it over and opened the battery compartment, intending to take out the batteries, but there weren't any in it.

"Hello, Eagle Eye," Hawkeye greeted Owen's dad through the walkie-talkie that shouldn't be working, "Did you miss me?"

Hearing his old nickname, spoken by a friend that had died decades ago, sent a chill up his spine.

HONORARY FAIRY

Once I heard my father start snoring, I knew it was safe to return to my room. However, before I did that, I cleaned up all of his empty beer bottles so he couldn't use that as an excuse to punish me in the morning.

"That looks painful," a little voice squeaked when I finally made it to my room.

Sitting on the ledge of my window was a pixie. She was about 6" tall with wings like a dragonfly.

"It is," I replied as I quietly closed the door behind me.

She was referring to the purple bruise around my left eye.

"What happened?" the pixie asked, flitting across the room to hover in front of me.

"The same thing that always happens," I deflected the question.

She knew about my father's temper. I don't know why she kept asking me to explain what happened every time she saw one of my bruises.

"What're you doing here?" I tried to change the subject, "You don't normally come here at night."

The pixie and I became friends months ago after I found her lying in the garden with a broken wing.

"I came to surprise you," she smiled.

"Surprise me how?"

In the past, her surprises had caused me more trouble than they were worth, like the time she brought me some candy, and my father found it and beat me because he thought I stole money from him to buy it.

"I went back to Arcadia and told them about how you saved me," she said.

Arcadia was the place where all fairies were from.

"And they voted to make you an honorary fairy," she smiled and flew around my head, "Isn't that great."

Somewhere in the house, I heard a door slam open.

"What the hell?" I heard my father grumble loudly from the living room.

I heard footsteps, lots of them. It sounded like a stampede.

I was about to go see what all the ruckus was when the pixie blocked my path.

"Don't go out there," she said.

"Why not?"

"Because it's not safe," she warned.

"OH MY GOD!" the muffled scream of my father came through the door. The last word trailed off into a choking garble.

"What's going on out there?"

"That," she jerked her tiny thumb over her shoulder, "Is a Red Cap feeding frenzy."

A Red Cap was a type of fairie that looked more like a goblin than a fairy. They were called Red Caps because they liked to color the caps they wore with blood.

The pixie had introduced me to one a couple of weeks ago.

"What're they doing here?" I asked.

"Helping you," she replied.

"I thought fairies couldn't help humans," I said.

That's what she told me when I first explained the reason for all of my bruises and asked her to help me.

Fairies can't involve themselves in human matters, she'd said.

"That was before we made you an honorary fairy," the pixie winked.

ALL THAT JAZZ

The bartender had just handed me a second bottle of beer when the jukebox started playing *Mack the Knife* by Bobby Darrin.

With beer in hand, I swiveled around on my stool, trying to see which of the bar's patrons had decided to play that song. I didn't see anyone.

"What kind of pansy plays a song like that in a bar like this?" I turned around to address the bartender. "Better yet, what is a song like that doing on the jukebox in a bar like this?" I added.

"A song like what?" the bartender asked.

"Like that," I hooked my thumb over my shoulder toward the jukebox.

The bartender raised her eyebrows as she looked from me to the jukebox.

"Don't tell me you like this song," I said, unable to keep my disdain from showing.

"I don't know what song you're talking about," she replied, "Because I don't hear anything."

"Are you shitting me?" I scoffed, "How can you not hear that?"

She shrugged, "I don't know what to tell you." She turned and walked away.

"Hey, Morris," I called out to the man cleaning glasses at the end of the bar, "Come here for a second."

Morris, who happened to be the owner of the place, set the towel and glass he was holding behind the bar and walked over to stand in front of me.

"What can I do for you, Albert?" Morris leaned on the bar and asked.

"You hear that, right?" I pointed my finger at the ceiling as if the music were a tangible thing hanging over my head.

"Hear what?" Morris looked up, confused at what I was pointing at.

"That song playing on the jukebox."

"There ain't no song playing on the jukebox, Albert. Not that any of us can hear." Morris kept his voice low and swept his eyes across the bar as he spoke.

"What's that supposed to mean?"

"I'll tell you what it means, but you're not going to like it," Morris said.

I gave him a confused look, "Why won't I like it?"

Five years ago," Morris began to tell me a story, "Jimmy Dagget was sitting right where you're sitting when he starts humming the tune to *Mack the Knife*. That old Bobby Darrin song. Later that night, he dropped dead of a heart attack. I didn't think anything of it until two years later when Thomas Flannery mentioned hearing that same song coming from the jukebox. A jukebox, I should add, that hasn't worked in over a decade. He died later that same night."

He let me mull over what he'd said before continuing.

"So, Albert, if you're telling me you're hearing *Mack the Knife*, coming from that jukebox," Morris pointed at the machine behind me, "Then I'm inclined to believe you because I don't believe in coincidences."

"Bullshit!" I spat.

"Bullshit or not," Morris said, "I'm going to need you to settle your tab before you leave."

THE PERFECT SHOT

"**H**arriet," Earl hissed, motioning for me to join him, "Come here."

I picked up my rifle and made my way over to where Earl was sitting, doing my best to stay low to the ground.

"Look," Earl whispered, pointing over the log we were hiding behind.

I lifted my head high enough to see what Earl was pointing at. When I saw the large buck grazing on the side of the hill about 200 yards away, I gasped.

"He's a big one," I said, ducking back out of sight so the deer wouldn't spot her.

"And he's all yours," Earl declared, "Assuming you can take the shot."

After pestering me for the better part of a year, I finally agreed to join Earl on one of his hunting trips.

"I can take the shot," I assured him.

I was no stranger to guns. I'd grown up around them and used to hunt regularly with my father and brothers when I was younger, but had given it up once I'd started high school. That was over fifteen years ago. I never told Earl about it, though.

I raised the rifle and rested it on the log, using the scope to line up my shot.

"You might have better luck if you get closer," Earl suggested.

I continued to line up my shot until I realized he was right. There were too many obstacles between me and the deer.

"If you can make it over to those rocks, you'll have a clear shot," Earl pointed at the collection of boulders between us and the deer.

"Maybe," I said, looking to see if there was a way for me to make it over to the boulders without giving myself away.

I found a path via a series of fallen trees and smaller rocks. I had to crawl most of the way, but I made it without spooking the deer.

When I looked back from my new position, Earl gave me a thumb's up.

It's show time, I thought, setting my rifle between two boulders and aiming it at the deer.

Bang! I said in my mind, pretending to go through with the shot. The truth was, I never had any intention of shooting the deer. I was just going through the motions, waiting for Earl to make his move.

BANG!

The crack of a rifle echoed through the forest. But the bullet that was intended for me never left the barrel of the gun. Earl's rifle had misfired, sending a piece of shrapnel right through his eye and into his brain.

I got up and walked back over to where Earl's body was, happy to see that the modifications I'd made to his rifle had worked as planned.

I knew he was going to try and kill me after I'd found the life insurance policy he'd taken out on me earlier that month.

"That's how you kill your spouse and make it look like a hunting accident," I said to Earl's corpse.

DÉJÀ VU

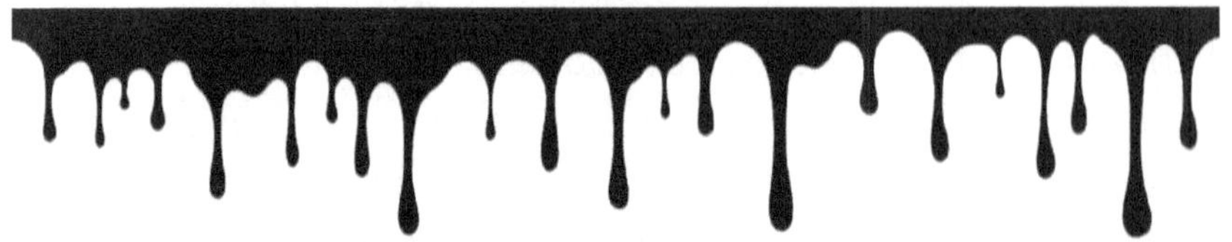

"So?" my husband, Todd, asked," What do you think?"

He'd just given me the tour of the vacation rental he'd surprised our family with.

"It's nice," I replied, "But it looks expensive."

"It wasn't, I promise," Todd smiled. "I was able to get it for half the usual rate because of a last-minute cancellation."

"Which room is mine?" our daughter, Caitlin, interrupted.

"You can have any room you want except for the one at the end of the hall," Todd answered, "That one belongs to mommy and me."

"Cool!" Caitlin declared, turning and running across the house to pick out a room.

Todd walked up behind me, pressing his body against mine as he wrapped his arms around my waist, "Why don't you go and check out the patio while I bring in the luggage?" he suggested.

"Maybe I will."

He kissed me on the cheek before leaving to retrieve our stuff from the car.

After Todd left, I walked over to the vertical blinds covering the sliding glass door and pulled on the cord, opening them.

"Wow," I gasped, staring at the large stone waterfall cascading into the pool that dominated the backyard, "This place is amazing."

I unlocked the sliding glass door and stepped out onto the patio so I could see the rest of the backyard. What I saw when I came around the corner of the house sent a shiver up my spine.

I rushed back inside.

When I saw my husband setting our bags on the floor, I stormed over to him. "I want to leave right now," I demanded.

"What?" Todd was confused by my sudden change in demeanor, "Why?"

I walked back outside and pointed at the pool toy, "That is why!"

Todd joined me, staring at the giant inflatable swan lying on the ground next to the pool, wondering why I was so upset about it.

"I don't understand," he said.

"My sister had one just like that," I explained, reminding him about how my sister had died in a tragic pool accident when we were kids.

"It's a common pool toy," he tried to placate me, "I'll put it in the garage so you don't have to look at it."

"Is this common too?" I walked over and pointed at the duct tape X's someone had put over the eyes. "My sister's had this too."

"I'm sorry," Todd apologized, "I didn't know it was going to be here, but I'll get rid of it immediately."

That's when Caitlin stepped outside with a towel draped over her shoulder.

"I love the new suit you bought me, mom!" she declared, "I can't wait to try it out!"

I looked over at her and gasped.

"Where'd you get that swim suit?" I snapped.

"On the bed where you left it for me."

"What's wrong now, honey?" Todd asked after seeing the distraught look on my face.

I pointed at Caitlin, "That's the same suit my sister was wearing the day she drowned."

OLD MAN IN THE WOODS

I was halfway through the woods when I first saw the old man.

That afternoon, I'd missed my bus, so I had to walk home. I was in the woods because cutting through them was a lot faster than following the streets.

I saw him before he saw me. When he turned around and noticed me looking at him, he looked surprised, like I had caught him doing something embarrassing.

Not wanting to intrude on his business, I turned my head away and kept on walking.

I saw him again the next time I was walking through the woods. He was dressed differently and loitering around a different area.

This time when he saw me, he gave a quick wave of his hand before going back to whatever it was that he was doing.

I returned the greeting and kept on walking.

I saw him three more times before I was finally forced to talk to him.

The fourth time I saw him, he stepped out from behind a tree blocking my path.

"Is your name Lee Austin?" he asked.

"Why do you want to know?" I eyed him suspiciously, wondering how he knew who I was.

"I was hoping you could help me with something," was his reply.

"With what?"

"It's better if I show you."

He started to walk off into the woods, but stopped when he realized I wasn't following him.

"I'm not going to hurt you," he said, "I doubt I could if I wanted to."

He was probably right about that. I was about six inches taller, a hundred pounds heavier, and over forty years younger than him, if I had to guess.

"It won't take long," he said, "It's just over by that log over there." He pointed.

I followed the man over to the log, keeping my distance in case he tried anything funny.

"Do you recognize that?" he asked, pointing at something sticking out from beneath the log.

"It looks like a piece of cloth," I said.

"What about that white part?" he gestured, "Does it look like it could be a letter?"

"I suppose," I agreed.

"Sort of looks like the one on your jacket." He looked up at me and pointed.

I looked down at the lettermen jacket I was wearing. "Yeah, I guess it does."

"Alright," the man said, "You can go now."
That was weird, I thought as I walked away.

———

The old man watched Lee Austin walk away. When he was out of earshot, he pulled out his phone and called his partner.

"Remember that football star that disappeared in the woods behind the high school five years ago?" he said.

"Yeah," his partner replied.

"I found his body."

"How'd you manage that?"

He looked over at Lee, watching as the teenager vanished from sight, something he'd seen him do every year for the past four years as he searched the woods for his body.

"I had a little help," the old man said.

HOME SWEET HOME

"Alright, close your eyes," my husband, Calvin, said to me after I'd gotten into the car and put on my seatbelt.

I turned to look at him. "Seriously?"

"Indulge me," he smiled, "I want this to be a surprise."

"Fine," I relented, closing my eyes, "But we better not be going far. You know how easily I get car sick."

When he pulled out of the apartment complex where we lived, I tried to figure out where he was going by keeping track of which way he turned. But I couldn't keep up. After about fifteen minutes of driving, I had no idea where we were. The only thing I was sure of was that we were nowhere near our apartment any longer.

"I hope we're getting close," I said, finally breaking my silence.

"Keep your eyes closed," he said. "We're almost there."

Almost to Calvin was another fifteen minutes of driving.

"Can I open them now?" I asked after hearing him put the car in park after coming to a stop.

"Not yet."

I heard him open his door, get out, and then shut it again. He opened my door a few moments later.

"Give me your hand," he said.

I held out my hand to let him lead me out of the car and onto what I assumed was a sidewalk. He stood behind me and turned me so that I was facing away from the street, then he covered my eyes with his hands to make sure I didn't peek until he was ready.

"Ready?" he asked.

"I was ready 30 minutes ago."

"Surprise!" he yelled, removing his hands, "I bought a house!"

"What! The! Fuck!"

"What's wrong?" Calvin asked, "Don't you like it?"

I was standing in front of my childhood home. The site where I endured years of sadistic abuse at the hands of my parents.

"This is impossible," I stammered.

The last time I saw the house was when I was 12. I stood in the same spot I was currently standing in and watched it burn to the ground. There shouldn't be anything left but an empty lot.

"This is not going how I planned," Calvin lamented.

I turned to look at him, "How did you find this place?"

"Don't get mad," he said, "But I reached out to your parents."

"My adoptive parents?"

"No," he shook his head, "I tracked down your real parents," he sighed heavily before continuing, "That was going to be my second surprise." He gestured weakly at the couple that had just walked out of the house.

I'd lied to Calvin and told him I never knew my birth parents. It was easier than telling him the truth.

My dad raised his hand and waved at me, "Welcome home Violet," he said with a smile on his face.

"We've missed you," my mom added.

Even though it had been 15 years since I burnt the house down around them, they hadn't aged a day.

PEEK A BOO

The creature killed her dad first.

She watched from her hiding place in the coat closet as it snuck up behind him. He was too busy cursing at the football game on the television to notice it approaching the recliner.

It reached around him with one of its spindly arms and used the long claw of its index finger to slice open his throat with a swift slashing motion of its hand.

Her dad jumped to his feet, clutching his neck as blood poured through his fingers. He tried to cry out, but the only sound that escaped his lips was a choked gurgle. He fell to the floor seconds later, dying with a confused look on his face.

The creature went after her mom next.

Her mom was in the kitchen cooking dinner when she heard the sound of her husband falling to the floor. Not knowing what the sound was, she walked into the living room to investigate.

"Honey?" she said as she walked into the room.

When her mom saw her dad's lifeless body lying in a pool of blood, she opened her mouth to scream. But the scream would never materialize.

The creature was hiding with its back pressed against the wall. When her mom walked by it, she had no clue it was standing there in the shadows.

As soon as her mom opened her mouth and drew in a breath to scream, the creature stepped in front of her and rammed a fist down her throat. When it pulled its fist free, her mom's heart was clutched in its hand.

That was when her older brother came down the stairs.

Seeing the grisly sight of his murdered parents, and the creature responsible for their deaths, he turned and tried to run back to his room, but the creature was much faster than him. It dropped the heart and grabbed her brother by the ankle, pulling him back down the stairs and lifting him into the air.

The boy struggled to free himself, but his struggles ended when the creature flung him against the wall with tremendous force, breaking his neck.

When the creature heard the boy wheeze, he flung him again.

She flinched when she heard the sound of her brother's bones snapping.

The creature examined the body of the boy, giving it a shake to make sure no life remained within it before tossing it aside.

She was all that remained. The rest of her family lay dead upon the floor.

The creature sniffed the air with its bulbous nose. Catching a scent, it walked over to the closet door where she was hiding. It reached out with its bloody hand, curling its fingers around the door handle, and pulled it open.

She stood there, looking up at the creature looming in the doorway. She wasn't afraid of it. She had no reason to be.

"The deed is done, little master," the creature growled, "What is your next command?"

THE WATERMELON PATCH

"Please, help yourself," Mrs. Wyatt, the homeowner, gestured at the plate of sliced watermelon on the counter. The motion made the collection of bracelets on her wrist jangle.

My husband, Aaron, and I were driving by on our way to meet our realtor at a different location when we saw the open house sign in Mrs. Wyatt's front yard and decided to stop.

Aaron, never one to turn down free food, picked up a large slice of watermelon and bit off a piece.

"Oh my god," he mumbled around a mouthful of pulp, "This is so good, you have to try it." He held the slice out to me.

Instead of taking the one he offered, I grabbed my own slice and took a bite.

"You're right," I said, taking a second bite. "It is good." I quickly finished the slice and took a second.

"Do you mind?" I held the second slice up to make sure it was okay with Mrs. Wyatt.

She shook her head, "Help yourself. I have plenty."

"Where'd you get it?" Aaron asked.

"It came from the garden in the backyard," Mrs. Wyatt gestured toward the sliding glass door, "Would you like to see it?"

"I would," I replied.

I was hoping to start my own garden once we found a house and thought about how much easier it would be if we bought a home that already had an established garden.

"After you," Mrs. Wyatt said, opening the door and stepping aside to let us walk out before her.

We walked over to the corner of the yard where various fruit and vegetable plants were thriving.

"The watermelon patch was the last thing I planted," Mrs. Wyatt said.

"Those are enormous," I gasped, walking over to look at the huge melons growing on the vines.

As I got closer, I stumbled over something sticking out of the ground. Aaron reacted quickly, grabbing hold of my shoulders to steady me.

"Are you okay?" he asked.

"Yeah," I replied, "I tripped over something."

We both looked down, shocked at what we saw protruding from the ground. It was more visible now because I had knocked it free when I tripped over it.

"Is that a hand?" I pointed at the skeletal remains.

"Yep," the husband replied.

That was when we noticed that the watermelon vines were growing out of a mound of dirt that was significantly higher than the surrounding area.

We both turned to look at Mrs. Wyatt for an explanation, but she had disappeared.

"Where did she go?" Aaron asked.

"This is going to sound insane," I said, "But I think that's her." I pointed at the hand. "Look at the bracelets on the wrist."

Even though they were crusted together with dirt, they were clearly the same bracelets Mrs. Wyatt was wearing when she greeted us at the door.

"What the hell are you two doing back here?" someone yelled from behind them.

We turned around and saw Mr. Wyatt standing on the back porch with a shovel in his hands.

CHARACTER ASSASSINATION

"**S**top typing!"

Startled by the angry voice of the man behind me, I jumped and instinctively did as he commanded.

I kept my hands away from the keyboard and didn't move as I waited to see what the intruder wanted.

"Turn around!"

I slowly swiveled in my chair until I was facing the man. When he came into view, I was shocked to see that he was dressed like the villain in the book I was working on. The one he had commanded me to stop writing.

He was also holding a long, serrated blade.

"Why're you dressed like that?" I asked.

The man looked down at his clothing briefly, "Like what?" He genuinely seemed confused, "This is the way I always dress."

"What I meant is, why are you dressed like a character from my book?" I clarified, "And how did you know what he looks like? I haven't even finished the story yet."

"Are you really that dense?" He gestured at me with the knife.

It took me a moment to figure out what he was implying.

"That's insane," I laughed even though I didn't find it funny. "There's no way you're him."

"And yet, here I am." He spread his arms a little.

This has to be a dream. Or maybe I'm dying and he's some kind of hallucination. Can a stroke cause you to have hallucinations?

Those and other thoughts raced through my mind.

"Let's assume you're real for a moment," I said, trying to wrap my brain around what was happening. "Why are you here?"

"To stop you from killing me."

Before he arrived, I was in the middle of writing the final confrontation between the hero and the villain. A confrontation where the villain was not meant to survive.

"I have to kill you... or rather the hero does," I insisted, "The story won't have the same impact if you survive."

I couldn't believe that I was actually taking the time to explain myself to a fictional character.

"You're the author," the villain said, "I'm sure you can find a way to make it work."

"I'm sorry," I turned back to my computer and started writing again, "This is the way it has to be."

He was just a figment of my imagination. I didn't think he could do anything to hurt me.

"I'm sorry too," the villain proclaimed, striding across the room and stabbing his knife through my hand, pinning it to the keyboard.

"WHAT THE FUCK!"

I yanked the knife out of the keyboard and stood up, cradling my injured hand to my chest.

"Looks like I owe you an apology," the villain said, gesturing at the hand he'd stabbed.

Confused by his change in demeanor, I looked down at my hand, shocked to see that the blood dripping from it was as black as ink.

"You're not the author of my story," he sounded surprised, "You're just another character in it."

BONNY

"Here you go," her mom said, setting the box of crayons and a few sheets of paper down on the coffee table. "That should keep you entertained until I'm done with my conference call."

"Okay, mommy," Louisa replied, taking a seat on the floor next to the table.

Her mom turned to leave, but Louisa stopped her.

"Wait," she said, "I forgot Bonny."

Bonny was Louisa's doll. It used to be her mom's doll, but she gave it to Louisa when they found it in an old box of toys at her grandmother's house.

"Hurry up and go get her," her mom said, gesturing towards the hall.

Louisa got up and ran to her room, returning a minute later with the doll. She sat on the floor again, setting Bonny down next to her.

"Do you have everything you need?" her mom asked.

Louisa nodded.

"Are you sure?"

"I'm sure," Louisa insisted.

"Do you need to go to the bathroom?"

Louisa shook her head, "I already went."

"Alright then. I'll be finished in thirty minutes," her mom said, "I want you to stay right here until I'm done. Got it?"

"Okay," Louisa agreed.

She waited until her mom turned and walked away before opening the box of crayons and selecting a color.

———

Twenty minutes later, her mom stepped out of the bedroom turned home office, and into the hall, thankful that the conference call had ended early.

When she peaked her head into the living room, she was happy to see Louisa still sitting on the floor in front of the coffee table coloring.

"How do you spell, Bonny?" she heard Louisa ask.

She was about to reply but stopped when her daughter began saying the letters.

"B, O, N, N, Y," Louisa spelled out the name, writing each letter as she said it.

When she was done, she turned the paper so that it was facing her doll.

"Did I spell it right?" she asked.

There was a moment of silence before Louisa spoke again.

"How do you spell that?" Louisa asked.

There was another moment of silence before Louisa began reciting another string of letters.

"C, E, E, C, E, E," she said, again writing each letter as she said it.

"What are you doing?" her mom snapped. The words came out a little more demanding than she'd intended.

Louisa turned around at the sound of her mother's voice, "Hi, mommy," she said, "Bonny wanted me to draw you a picture."

She held up the drawing, which featured a large heart inside which were the names BONNY + CEECEE

"Do you like it?"

No, she thought, *I don't like it*.

She hated the name Ceecee. It was what her younger sister, Bonita, used to call her when they were growing up because she couldn't say Cecelia.

There was no way Louisa could have known about that because Bonita had died over 20 years ago.

THE OMEN

My son, Dante, left his door open a crack.

I stood in the hall and watched through the narrow opening as he slid something under his bed.

"What's that?" I pushed the door open and stepped into the room.

"Nothing," he sputtered, quickly getting to his feet.

"That doesn't look like nothing," I pointed at the edge of the box that was barely visible beneath his bed.

"It's just some stuff I found," Dante replied.

I could tell he was being evasive because he wouldn't look me in the eye when he spoke.

"Let me see it." I held my hand out.

He looked like he was trying to come up with an excuse not to but thought better of it when I snapped at him.

"Now!" I demanded.

Reluctantly, he dropped to his knees, slid the box out from beneath the bed, and held it out to me.

The stench of what was inside wafted up to my nose as I took it from him.

"Where did you get these?" I held the open box out to him so he could see the relatively fresh carcasses of the three dead crows inside.

"Outside," Dante said, "But I didn't kill them. They were already dead."

Before I could reply, something slammed against the bedroom window, rattling it loudly.

"That's probably another one," Dante said.

He was right, I could see the smudge mark in the shape of a bird pressed against the glass and a single black feather fluttering to the ground.

"They've been doing that since you brought Corbin home," he said.

Corbin was Dante's newborn baby brother who I'd brought home from the hospital the day before. Technically, they were half-brothers since Dante's father was killed shortly after he was conceived.

I closed the box and handed it back to him. "You don't have to hide stuff like this from me," I said.

"You're not mad?" he sounded surprised.

"Of course not," I tousled his hair with my hand.

"I can keep them?"

"Yes, you can," I smiled, "But you should probably keep them in the garage. At least until they stop stinking."

"Okay," he agreed.

"You know," I said, "The death of a crow is considered a good omen."

"Really? My teacher told me it was a bad omen."

"Not in this house, it's not." I decided to let him in on a family secret, "Stay right here." I held my palm out. "I'll be right back."

I went to my room, retrieved the box I kept in the closet, and carried it back to Dante's room where I showed him the dried-out crow carcasses inside.

"Where'd you get those?" he asked.

"I collected them the day I brought you home. That's how I knew you were special."

"Special how?" Dante asked.

I fingered the upside-down cross around my neck and thought about the promise of power that was made to me when I killed Dante's father.

"You'll have to wait and see."

FOR THE RECORD

Courtney walked into the room cradling a cardboard box in her arms.

"Look what I found up in the attic," she said, sliding the box onto the dining room table in front of me.

She reached inside the box and pulled out an old vintage rock and roll album that was in near pristine condition.

"Oh my god," I gasped, "You found Dad's old record collection. I'd forgotten about it."

Our father had recently passed away. We were going through his belongings, trying to decide what we wanted to keep and what we wanted to sell.

The records were a big deal in our family because nobody but our father was allowed to play them. He used to lock himself in his room whenever he would listen to them. Which was something he would do at least once a week.

"Where's the record player?" I asked, "We have to play one just to spite him."

"I think I saw it in the closet of the spare bedroom," Courtney said, "I'll go get it."

She slid the album she was holding back into the box before walking to the back of the house. When she returned, she found me flipping through the albums.

"We should look these up on eBay," I suggested, "See if they're worth anything."

"I wouldn't be surprised if they are," Courtney replied as she set the record player down on the table and plugged it in. "They're in perfect condition."

"Which one should we listen to first?" I asked.

I was holding up two albums from bands she recognized, one was Queen, the other was Aerosmith.

"Queen," Courtney replied, "Definitely Queen."

I started to slide the record out of its sleeve. As I did, a polaroid fell out.

Courtney picked up the photo and looked at it. It featured a young, scantily clad woman smiling at the camera. Written at the bottom of the photo was the name Elaine Moore.

"Who the hell is this?" Courtney held up the photo so I could see it, "You don't think dad was cheating on mom when he went on those business trips, do you?"

I looked inside the Aerosmith album and found another photo of a different woman.

We then checked the rest of the albums, finding a different photo in all thirty of them.

Courtney picked up her phone.

"What are you doing?" I asked.

"Checking Facebook to see if I can find out anything about these women," Courtney replied, "I want to know why dad has pictures of them hidden in his albums."

I thought that sounded like a good idea, so I picked up my phone and decided to search for one of the names on google.

"I don't think you're going to find them on Facebook," I said after seeing the first result of my google search.

"Why not?" Courtney asked.

"Because I think they're all dead," I showed Courtney the newspaper headline I'd clicked on:

LOCAL WOMAN BELIEVED TO BE 19TH VICTIM OF UNIDENTIFIED SERIAL KILLER, the headline read.

SUMMER CAMP

I crawled out from beneath the bed and crept over to the window.

"What're you doing?" Wally hissed.

The two of us had run into the camp counselor's cabin to hide from the Serenity Lake Slasher who was going from cabin to cabin slaughtering campers.

We figured we'd be safe in the counselor cabin because the slasher had already been inside as was evident from the mutilated bodies of the three counselors lying on the floor.

"It's been a while since we've heard anything," I whispered, pulling the curtains aside so I could look out across the campground. "I think he might be gone."

I scanned the area, looking for any sign of movement, but I didn't see anything other than the trail of bodies the killer had left behind.

Wally reluctantly crawled out of his hiding place and made his way over to the window.

"How long have we been in here?" he asked, keeping his voice low.

"About an hour," I replied.

"Only an hour?" Wally sighed, "It felt longer than that."

"What do you think we should do?" I asked.

"Nothing," Wally replied quickly. "I think we should just stay here and wait until help arrives."

"It's three o'clock in the morning," I pointed out. "If help is coming, it won't be coming any time soon."

"What do you suggest we do?" he snapped back.

"I think one of us should run over to the director's office and use the phone to call the police," I suggested.

"You're welcome to try," Wally said, "But I'm not going anywhere."

"Fine." I declared, "I will."

I walked over to the door of the cabin and eased it open a crack so I could peek outside.

"You're nuts," Wally shook his head in disbelief. "You're going to get yourself killed."

"No, I won't," I insisted.

"How can you be so sure?" Wally was amazed at how cocky I sounded.

"Because the killer's not looking for me," I smiled, "He's looking for you."

"Why would he be looking for me and not you?"

"Because I'm the one who found him and brought him back to life."

I swung the cabin door open and stepped aside so Wally could see the Serenity Lake Slasher standing in the doorway.

"He's all yours," I swept my arm towards Wally.

The slasher stepped into the cabin and raised his machete.

Wally tried to escape, but he wasn't fast enough.

"That was the last one," I said once the slasher had dispatched Wally. "Time for you to go."

The slasher dropped his head in sorrow, unhappy that the evening's festivities had come to an end.

"Sorry," I apologized.

I reached up and removed the mask from the slasher's face. As I did, his body dissolved until there was nothing left but bones. Those bones then clattered to the floor.

"I doubt my parents will send me to summer camp next year," I said to the bones, "But if they do, you're coming with me."

PRECIOUS PONIES

"I'm a Precious Pony, you're a Precious Pony, we're a Precious Pony fam-i-ly!" Lily sang from the living room.

I was sitting in my home office, trying to reconcile some business accounts when I heard my daughter singing.

It didn't bother me at first, in fact, I thought it was cute initially. But by the start of Lily's sixth rendition of the Precious Ponies theme song, I'd had enough.

"Margaret!" I yelled.

When my wife didn't answer, I got up and opened the office door to yell out into the hall, "Margaret!" I repeated.

"What?" my wife eventually called back, appearing at the end of the hall with a full laundry basket in her arms.

"Where were you?" I snapped.

Margaret looked down at the basket of clothes she was holding, indicating that should have been answer enough.

"In the laundry room," she snapped back.

"Can you please do something about your daughter?" I gestured towards the living room where Lily had started a new verse of Precious Ponies, "I've got to get these reconciliations done tonight and I can't think straight with her singing like that."

Margaret released an exasperated sigh as she set the laundry basket on the floor and stormed off into the living room.

I waited until I heard my wife's voice say, "Lily, honey, daddy is trying to work and needs you to be quiet."

I expected that to be the end of it, but it wasn't. Lily started singing the song again as soon as her mother finished speaking.

That pissed me off. What angered me even more was when my wife started to sing along to the song with Lily.

"I'm a Precious Pony, you're a Precious Pony, we're a Precious Pony fam-i-ly!" they sang in unison.

I stormed into the living room, "What the hell is wrong with you?" I yelled at my wife, "You were supposed to stop her, not encourage her."

My wife didn't respond, she just kept on singing with Lily. That was when I noticed that the two of them were staring at the television as they sang, but there wasn't anything playing on the screen. It was showing nothing but static.

I walked around the couch and stood in front of them.

I pointed my finger at my wife and was about to yell at her, but what I saw made me drop my hand and take two steps back. My anger was instantly forgotten and quickly replaced with concern.

What's wrong with their eyes? I thought.

I couldn't make sense of what I was seeing. Where their eyes should have been was nothing but a field of static.

I tried to look away but found that I couldn't. I was frozen in place. I tried to open my mouth to call for help, but I couldn't speak the words. The only thing I could do was join the chorus with my wife and daughter.

"I'm a Precious Pony," I sang.

LITTLE RED RIDING HOOD

"Your grandfather called," my mom said as I walked into the house. "Your grandmother had another bad night and now he needs some help."

I didn't even have time to take my backpack off before she ambushed me.

"Do I have to go?" I whined.

"Yes, you do, Molly," she insisted. "He helped us when we needed it, now we need to help him."

My grandmother had been confined to a bed for the past 5 years. Up until recently, my mom had been the one to go help my grandfather when he called, but now that I was 16, she was making me help him instead.

"Fine." I dropped my backpack onto the floor before storming back outside to get my bike.

My grandparents lived on a farm at the edge of town, which was a three-mile bike ride for me. Thankfully, I only had to ride to their house. My grandfather always gave me a ride back in his truck.

———

My grandfather was standing on the porch when I rode up the gravel-lined drive. He waved at me when he saw me, and I waved back.

"Hey, Pawpaw," I greeted as I leaned my bike against the porch, "Mom said you needed help again."

"I do," he admitted. "I'm sorry to keep calling on you like this."

"It's okay," I lied, "I don't mind."

"A kid your age shouldn't have to deal with this shit," he said. He didn't have any qualms about cussing around me, "I don't know why your mother keeps sending you instead of coming herself."

"I think she's having a hard time dealing with all of this," I offered as an excuse.

My grandmother's condition had been deteriorating the past few months, which was why she was having so many bad days lately.

"Come on around back and let's get started," he gestured for me to follow as he walked around the side of the house.

He was leading me to the large barn at the back of the property that at one time used to house the livestock my grandparents raised.

That was before my grandmother got sick. Nothing lived in it now.

I followed my grandfather to the back of the barn, where he had a tarp laid out. When he lifted the tarp, I gasped.

"Holy shit," I said.

There were three mutilated corpses beneath the tarp.

"Holy shit, indeed," my grandfather agreed.

"She really did have a bad night," I declared.

Normally, when my grandmother had a bad night, she only killed one person. That was usually enough to satisfy her hunger.

"Why do you think she did this?" I gestured at the bodies.

"I think the wolf inside her knows she's dying and wants to make the most of the time it has left," he explained.

That made sense.

"Did you buy more lye?" I asked, grabbing one of the shovels leaning against the barn, "You were getting kind of low last time I was here."

ALEXA

Thomas was sitting on the couch, watching TV, when the blue ring on the smart speaker lit up.

Thomas could see it because it was sitting on the TV stand right next to the TV.

"Now playing, *Don't Fear the Reaper*, by Blue Oyster Cult," the speaker announced in its pleasant feminine voice.

The familiar guitar intro to the song began playing a moment later. It was louder than the TV.

"Alexa, stop playing," Thomas snapped at the device.

"Okay," Alexa replied.

The music abruptly cut off.

Thomas rewound his show a couple of minutes so he could rewatch the scene he'd miss when the smart speaker had started playing.

As soon as he restarted his show, the blue ring lit up again as the speaker announced, "Now playing, *I Just Died in Your Arms Tonight*, by Cutting Crew."

The haunting sound of the song's opening keyboard began to play. Once again, it was louder than the TV.

"Alexa, stop playing!" Thomas shouted.

"Okay," Alexa replied, ending the song.

"Stupid thing," Thomas muttered to himself.

He didn't really like the smart speaker. It was his wife's. She'd placed it in the living room so she could listen to music while she cleaned the house.

"Now playing *Last Kiss* by J Frank Wilson and the Cavaliers," Alexa suddenly announced.

"Are you freaking kidding me," Thomas complained as the opening drumbeat began thumping through the speaker.

"ALEXA! STOP! PLAYING!"

Thomas could feel his face heat up as he yelled at the device.

"Okay," she joyfully replied as the music cut off.

Thomas picked up the remote and rewound the show for the second time.

"Now playing," Alexa began to announce.

"Don't you fucking dare!" Thomas yelled at the device. But she ignored him.

"*If Tomorrow Never Comes* by Garth Brooks," she finished.

The twang of a country guitar came through the speakers.

"That's it!" Thomas jumped to his feet. "I've had enough of your shit!"

He stalked across the room, intending to unplug the annoying device, but he only got a few steps before a sharp pain lanced through his chest, stopping him.

Oh my god! he thought, *I think I'm having a heartache.*

The next jolt of pain brought him to his knees as he clutched his chest, gasping for breath.

"Help," he tried to call out, but the sound of the music drowned out his voice.

Feeling light-headed and unable to get his limbs to obey him, Thomas collapsed to the floor.

He tried to crawl back to the couch where he'd left his phone, but he didn't get very far.

Before he blacked out, the last thing he saw was the power strip sticking out from behind the TV.

"It's not plugged in," he wheezed out his final words as he noticed the echo plug lying on the carpet next to the power strip.

The smart speaker stopped playing the same moment that Thomas took his last breath.

75

RUBY

"Have you seen, Ruby?" I asked my husband, "She said she wanted to go to the store with me, but I can't find her anywhere."

"Have you looked outside," he replied, "Last time I saw her she was sitting on the dock."

Behind our house was a large pond.

I sighed when my husband told me that was where Ruby was. The only time she went down to the pond was when she was having boy trouble.

"I guess I better go and talk to her," I said.

Ruby turned around to look behind her when she heard my shoes slap against the wooden planks of the dock.

"You okay?" I asked when I saw my daughter's tear-streaked cheeks.

"I'm fine," Ruby replied, wiping her nose with the back of her hand.

"Want to tell me what happened?"

"Boys suck," Ruby cursed.

"You're going to have to be a little more specific than that," I prodded, trying to get her to open up.

"Zach broke up with me this morning at school," Ruby sobbed.

"Why did he do that?" I asked, taking a seat on the dock beside her. "I thought that everything was going great between the two of you."

"It was," Ruby agreed, "Until Candace convinced him that I had something to do with Ryan's disappearance," she sniffled, "And that if he didn't want the same thing to happen to him, he should stop seeing me."

Ryan was Ruby's boyfriend the previous year. He'd disappeared months ago under suspicious circumstances, and nobody had seen him since.

"Why would she say that?" I wanted to get a little more information from her before I started worrying.

"Everyone knows I was the last person to see Ryan before he disappeared," Ruby said. "It's only a matter of time before they figure out what happened to him."

"Nobody is going to find out about what happened to Ryan," I insisted. "Not as long as you stick to the story."

I placed her arm around Ruby's shoulders.

"Everything will be fine," I said. "Zach will be back. You'll see."

"No, he won't," Ruby replied.

"Sure, he will," I insisted. "You just need to give him some time to come to his senses and realize how unhappy he is without you. In the meantime, you need to keep a level head don't do anything rash."

"It's too late for that," Ruby sighed as she gestured at the placid surface of the pond.

"Seriously, Ruby," I snapped.

Zach's lifeless eyes were looking up at me from the bottom of the pond.

"Go get your father and then go to your room," I jabbed my finger back toward the house, "You're grounded."

THE ATTIC

Tammy was in the attic, looking for some old toys, when she accidentally knocked over a stack of boxes. When she turned around to survey the damage she'd done, she saw an old steamer trunk.

"Where'd that come from?" she muttered to herself.

She quickly moved all of the boxes out of the way so she could kneel in front of the trunk before opening it.

As soon as she lifted the lid, a musty stench wafted out at her. When she saw the bones stacked inside, she slammed the lid shut.

"MOM!" she yelled.

She continued to call for her mother until she heard footsteps stomping up the attic steps.

"What are you doing up here?" her mother asked, "You know we don't like it when you kids come up here. And why were you screaming like that?"

"I was looking for some of my old Precious Pony toys to give to April's sister when I found that." Tammy pointed at the old steamer trunk.

"What about it?" her mother asked.

"Look inside," Tammy insisted.

Her mother walked over and lifted the lid. She looked at the contents for a moment before closing it and turning back to face her daughter.

"That's just some of your father's old Halloween decorations," her mother replied. "I told him to get rid of them ages ago, but I guess he didn't listen."

"They're not real?" Tammy asked.

"Of course they're not," her mom smiled.

"That's a relief," Tammy sighed.

Later, after Tammy had gone over to her friend's house, her mother picked up the phone and called her husband.

"What the hell were you thinking?" she hissed into the phone.

"What are you talking about?" her husband asked.

"The skeletons in the attic," she said, "I thought you'd gotten rid of them."

"I was going to," he replied, "But I never got around to it."

"Well, Tammy found them."

"Crap," her husband sighed, "I guess that means it's time to get the heck out of Dodge."

The next morning, Tammy's little brother woke her up to tell her that their parents were gone.

"What do you mean gone?" she asked him.

"They packed up the car and left."

Wondering if her parents leaving had anything to do with the skeletons, Tammy went back up to the attic and examined the bones.

"These aren't fake," she said and then went downstairs to call the police.

A month later, a detective brought Tammy down to the station to talk to her.

"We've gotten the DNA results back on those two skeletons you found in the attic and were able to positively ID them," the detective said.

"Who were they?" Tammy asked.

"That's what I wanted to talk to you about," the officer said. "You said you found the skeletons the day before your parents disappeared, right?"

"That's right," Tammy agreed.

"I don't see how that's possible." The officer slid the DNA results across the table to her. "Because it was your parents' skeletons that were in that trunk."

WE ALL SCREAM FOR ICE CREAM

"What do you think they're hiding back there?" I asked, gesturing at the 12ft tall barbed wire fence.

"That's what we're going to find out," Hayley smiled conspiratorially as she positioned the bolt cutters to cut through a section of the chain-link fence.

Haley was moving in a couple of days and had talked me into going with her to find out what the town was hiding behind the fenced-in area.

One last hurrah, Haley had called it.

"Hurry up," I hissed.

It was taking Hayley way too long to cut through the fence.

The area was patrolled regularly by the sheriff's office and if she didn't hurry, we were sure to get caught.

"I've almost got it," Hayley grunted, trying and failing to exert enough pressure to cut through the links.

"Here," I reached out for the cutters, "Let me do it." As the pitcher for the high school softball team, I had more upper body strength than Hayley.

"You go, Wonder Woman," Hayley said as I easily snipped through the fence and pulled it back, creating a space large enough for us to squeeze through.

"Shut up and crawl through before somebody sees us," I urged.

Hayley did as she was told, and I followed closely behind her.

On the other side of the fence was a densely wooded area. We walked through the trees until we came to a small clearing.

"That's it?" Hayley sounded disappointed.

In the clearing was a dilapidated brick building with a sign in front of it that featured the rusty and faded logo of an ice cream shop.

"Looks like it," I said as we approached the building.

"Well, that sucks," Haley sighed. "I was expecting something a lot more interesting than that." She gestured at the building.

"Like what?"

"Like some sort of secret government installation," Hayley replied.

"Here, in this shithole of a town?" I scoffed.

Haylcy reached down and picked up a loose chunk of asphalt from what remained of the Ice Cream shop's parking lot and chucked it through the opening where the shop's window once was.

"Fuck this town," she declared as the piece of asphalt rattled around inside the dilapidated shop.

A moment later, a rusty ice cream scoop came flying out at us, landing with a clatter at our feet.

"I think it's time to go," I said.

Apparently, we weren't the only people in the restricted area.

"I think you're right," Hayley agreed.

We both turned to leave, but stopped when we saw the man standing behind us.

He was wearing a white uniform with spatters of blood across it. In his hands he was holding two ice cream cones that were topped with some type of unidentifiable lumps of flesh.

Flies buzzed around the cones.

"You can't leave," the man smiled, showing his perfect, white, teeth, "You haven't tried the flavor of the week yet."

"I think we just found out why this place is off limits," I whispered.

THE JOB

"What do you think so far?" Jeff asked.

He'd been explaining what my daily duties would be as the overnight security guard for the mannequin factory.

"Honestly," I replied, "I feel like I'm going to be overpaid."

Jeff laughed. "You might change your mind once I take you out onto the factory floor." He gestured at the double doors upon which was a sign that said: AUTHORIZED PERSONNEL ONLY.

I doubt that, I thought.

"Here," Jeff reached into the pocket of his uniform and pulled out two pairs of mirrored sunglasses. "Put these on." He held one of the pairs out to me.

I waited until Jeff put his on before I put on mine.

"Ready?" He unlocked the double doors.

I nodded, "I'm ready."

"After you," Jeff opened the door and gestured for me to enter the factory floor before him.

"Wow, that's a lot of mannequins," I said.

There were hundreds of them, lined up in rows like soldiers in formation.

"The first thing you want to do when you come in here is lock the door behind you," Jeff said. "Once you've done that, your real job begins."

"My real job?" I asked for clarification.

Jeff smiled. "You'll see," he replied cryptically.

At that point, I got the sudden feeling that I was being set up for a practical joke.

"You take that row," Jeff pointed at the space between mannequins to my right, "And I'll take this one." he pointed to the left.

I started walking down the aisle between mannequins.

"Am I supposed to be looking for something?" I asked.

He hadn't told me why we were walking the floor.

"You'll know it when you see it," Jeff replied.

We had almost made it to the opposite side of the factory floor when I caught movement out of the corner of my eye.

I turned my head and found one of the mannequins looking in my direction. It had been looking the other way a moment ago.

I continued to stare at the mannequin.

When it blinked, I cried out and backed away from it, knocking into the mannequin behind me which knocked into another, causing a domino effect of falling mannequins.

The mannequin that had blinked took off running toward the double doors.

"That's what you're looking for," Jeff pointed at the mannequin that was desperately trying to open the locked doors.

"Is that thing real?" I asked, my heart pounding in my chest.

"It's real," Jeff explained, walking over and offering me a hand to help me back to my feet. "More real than it's supposed to be. That's why it's our job to flush them out. That's what the mirrored sunglasses are for," he tapped the lenses, "They can't resist looking at their reflection."

"What're we supposed to do now?" I asked.

"Put it down before it escapes and hurts someone," Jeff replied.

When he saw the way I was looking at him, he smirked and said, "Still think you're being overpaid?"

CAPTIVATION STREET

"What're you doing?" I asked.

My wife, Violet, was sitting backward with her knees on the couch, peeking out through the gap in the curtains.

"Waiting," Violet replied.

"For what?" I walked over so I could see through the gap.

"For that," she pointed at the car that was slowly driving down the street.

I watched the SUV cruise by the house. I could see two people sitting in the front. The driver, who was a dark-haired man wearing sunglasses, and the passenger, a light-haired woman.

The couple, I assumed they were married, were looking back and forth across the street as if they were searching for something.

"Did you see the kid in the backseat?" Violet asked.

"No," I replied, "I didn't." All of the rear windows were tinted, so I'd focused my attention on the people in the front.

"I saw her press her face to the window as they drove by," she said.

"A kid is the last thing we need around here," I sighed.

Before my wife could reply, the phone on the end table began ringing, interrupting us.

"Hello," I said, after lifting the receiver from its cradle.

"Did you see the car?" Marcus asked. Marcus was our neighbor from across the street.

"Yeah, we saw it," I said.

"What do you think?" Marcus was asking about the couple in the front seat.

"It's hard to think anything without talking to them first," I replied.

"I suppose you're right," he agreed.

"Did you see the kid?" I asked.

"They have a kid with them?" Marcus sounded surprised.

"Yep," I said. "Violet saw her when they drove by."

"How old?"

I lowered the phone so I could talk to Violet. "How old did she look?" I asked her.

"10, maybe 12, somewhere around that age," she answered.

I relayed the answer to Marcus.

"They're coming back around," Violet announced when she saw the car again.

"Do you want to go outside and talk to them, or should I?" I asked Marcus.

"Definitely you," Marcus chuckled, "We don't want to scare them."

Marcus was a large, muscular man who looked like he could be the leader of a motorcycle gang.

"Wish me luck?" I said before hanging up the phone and walking out of the house to stand on my porch.

The SUV suddenly stopped when the man driving saw me standing outside.

I raised my hand in greeting and walked down to the curb.

The woman sitting in the passenger seat rolled down her window as I approached.

"Excuse me," she said, "Could you tell us how to get to the interstate? We seem to be lost."

"You're not lost," I replied. "You're stuck on Captivation Street like the rest of us. If you want to come inside, I can explain everything to you." I gestured at the house.

The couple chose to continue driving and ended up traveling down the same street three more times before they finally gave up and pulled into my driveway.

THE LOBOTOMY CHALLENGE

"**I**s everyone ready?" the masked teenager in the hoody asked. He was standing on a stack of pallets, speaking through a handheld electronic device to disguise his voice.

"Let's do this!" someone in the gathered crowd yelled out. Several others joined in, calling out their eagerness to begin.

There were about a hundred teenagers gathered in the old warehouse on the outskirts of town. Of them, only the thirty kids who were invited were there to take part in The Lobotomy Challenge. The rest were there to watch and record the insane event.

"The Lobotomy Challenge is a test of endurance," the masked teenager announced. "Whoever lasts the longest wins the prize." He gestured at the overstuffed bag of cash sitting near his feet.

On the floor in the center of the warehouse were thirty specially designed hollow wooden boxes. The boxes were about 4" thick and 8" wide. Sticking out of the top of each were two rows of nails with the points up.

"Take your positions," the masked teenager said.

Each contestant knelt before one of the boxes. Many of them bragged about how they were going to be the ones to win.

"Begin," he announced.

Each contestant assumed a push-up position over their box with their eyes centered over the rows of nails. That was the required position to take part in the challenge. They were expected to hold that position as long as possible or forfeit. The winner was the one who stayed in position the longest.

The masked teenager waited five minutes, making sure everyone was in position before he pulled out a small handheld remote.

I told you I'd get my revenge one day. He thought as he looked out at the group of boys and girls who'd tormented him earlier that year.

He would never forget how they had blindfolded him, tore off all of his clothes, and then shackled him to one of the lunch tables in the cafeteria right before the bell rang. They'd even poured a bottle of vegetable oil over his body so he would flail around as he struggled to free himself.

They'd done it simply because he was perceived as different, not normal by their standards.

All the kids who'd taken part or laughed at him were now lined up on the warehouse floor before him.

The masked teenager pressed the button on the remote, releasing the reservoir of oil that was hidden in the center of each wooden box. It was a special type of oil, designed to flow quickly.

By the time the contestants realized what was happening, it was too late. The oil flowed under their hands, making it impossible for them to hold themselves up.

The crowd screamed and ran as the contestants began to slip and fall, impaling their faces on the nails sticking out of the boxes.

The masked teenager lifted the voice changer to his mouth and said, "I win," before picking up the bag of cash and hopping off the stack of pallets to leave.

SPECIAL DELIVERY

"**G**ood morning, Ms. Stevenson," Nurse Barbara announced as she entered the room. "I've got a surprise for you," she smiled, lingering in the doorway as she waited for me to respond.

I'd never seen Nurse Barbara before and only knew her name because of the badge that was clipped to her uniform.

"A surprise?" I repeated.

I had no idea what she could be referring to and at that point, I didn't care. My pain medication was starting to wear off and the incision where they'd removed the tumor from my abdomen was starting to burn.

"I hope it's drugs," I said, only half joking.

"Oh, this is better than that," Nurse Barbara smiled, ducking out into the hall and returning with a bassinet.

"Is that a baby?" I pointed at the swaddled form lying in the bassinet. I couldn't see it very well from where I was lying, but I assumed that's what it was.

I'd decided long ago that I didn't want kids of my own, so I wasn't thrilled at having someone else's kid wheeled into my room. Especially after I just had surgery a few hours earlier.

"This adorable little thing is more than just a baby." Nurse Barbara lifted the newborn and cradled it in her arms as she carried it over to me, "It's your baby."

"The hell it is," I spat the words at her.

Nurse Barbara tried to hand the baby to me, but I refused to take it.

"It's yours," the smile dropped from her face as she lowered her voice and spoke firmly to me, "You have to take it."

"No, I don't," I folded my arms over my chest and turned away from her, "You need to take it back to wherever it came from."

"A baby like this can't be given back." Nurse Barbara said as she set the infant back in the bassinet and then wheeled it next to my bed, "Once it's been delivered, it's yours."

"I didn't deliver any baby," I shoved the bassinet toward her, "I've never even been pregnant."

"Are you sure about that?" Nurse Barbara slowly wheeled the bassinet back toward me, unwrapping the blanket that covered the baby as she walked.

Once the blanket was removed, the writhing black mass of a cancer tumor was revealed. A tumor that looked vaguely like a baby.

I woke with a scream.

"Oh good, you're awake," Nurse Sarah, my regular nurse, said when she heard me cry out, "It's time for your pain medication."

"I had the worst nightmare," I panted, wiping sweat from my brow. "I dreamt that a nurse brought a baby into my room, but it wasn't really a baby. It was the tumor the doctor removed, and it was moving around like it was still alive."

"Oh, that wasn't a dream," Nurse Sarah said, stepping out of the way so I could see the bassinet and the black mass of flesh lying inside it sucking on a bottle.

CONTINUE GAME?

"How much for the Playstation?" I pointed at the console in the display case.

"The what?" the old guy behind the counter asked.

"The PlayStation," I repeated, "Under those comics."

The old guy opened the case and set the stack of comics to the side, "This thing?" He picked up the console.

"Yeah."

He pulled it out of the case and examined it.

"Five bucks," he declared

"Does it work?" I wasn't going to waste money on a broken console.

He shrugged, "If it doesn't you can bring it back."

"Okay." I pulled out my wallet.

When I got home, I hooked the console up to the television.

"Please work." I pushed the power button.

YES!

I couldn't help but smile when I saw the Sony logo appear on the screen.

The fact that the console powered on was great news, but that was just the first step in seeing if it worked. The next step was seeing if it would run a game.

Luckily, I had a few of my dad's old game discs that he gave me years ago. I'd forgotten about them until I saw the PlayStation in the second-hand shop. I was about to go get them, but I stopped when I saw a strange prompt on the TV.

The words: CONTINUE GAME? Y/N had replaced the start-up screen.

I checked the PlayStation after I bought it. I knew there wasn't a game inside it.

Curious about why it was asking me to continue, I picked up the controller, selected the letter Y, and pushed the X button.

The television started flashing. The flashes were so bright that I had to cover my eyes. When it finally stopped and I was able to see again, I found that I was no longer in my apartment. I was in a basement furnished with nothing but a dirty mattress, a bucket, and my television with the PlayStation still attached to it.

"What the hell?" I stood up. As I did, I heard something clink. That's when I noticed a pressure around my ankle.

What the fuck!

There was a shackle around my left leg. Attached to it was a chain that was fastened to a support beam several feet away.

I think I might be losing my mind.

I had no idea how I ended up where I was.

When I turned back and looked at the TV, I noticed that new words had appeared on the screen. This is what it said:

It is 1998. You are Shannon Hughes. You are being held captive. You have 3 days to escape.

Below that was a timer.

The sound of several deadbolts being unlocked drew my attention to the stairs leading out of the basement. I heard a door open and then a man descended the steps. Even though he looked

25 years younger, I immediately recognized the old man from the second-hand shop.

"Hello, Shannon," he smiled. "It's time to show you why you're here."

HELPING HAND

"Excuse me?" A man's voice called out.

Since I was the only person in the area, I assumed whoever I'd heard was talking to me, so I stopped and turned around to see what they wanted. But, after I did, I didn't see anyone.

"Down here," the man said.

I followed the sound of the voice to an uncovered manhole a few feet away. Standing at the bottom of the hole was a man dressed in a business suit.

"Hi," the man waved when he saw me standing on the curb above him, "Thanks for stopping."

"What're you doing down there?" I asked.

"Admitting this is so embarrassing," he said, "But I'm stuck. Been stuck for over an hour. I thought I could climb back out, but I can't."

"Why'd you go down there in the first place?"

"I dropped my phone," he held up the device so I could see it as he explained, "There was no way I was going to just leave it down here."

"That sucks," I sympathized.

"It really does," he agreed. "That's why I need your help getting out."

"Why didn't you just call 911 and tell them where you were?" He had a phone. That's what I would've done if I were in his situation.

"I would've," he said, "If the phone was working." He showed me the black screen. "Something must've happened to it when it fell."

"I suppose I can call them for you," I offered, pulling my phone out of the inside pocket of my suit.

"I'd preferred if you didn't," he replied, "Being stuck down here is embarrassing enough. The fewer people who know about it the better."

"I don't know how else I can help you," I said.

"If you could just give me a helping hand," he reached his hand up toward me, "I'll be able to climb out with no problem."

I looked around, seeing if there was anyone else who might be better suited to helping the man but there was nobody else around.

"Two minutes of your time," he said. "That's all it will take."

"Okay," I sighed.

I would've preferred pawning off the guy's rescue on someone else, but since there wasn't anyone else around, I was going to have to do it myself.

After squatting next to the hole, I leaned forward and reached my hand out to him.

"Thanks, Roger," the man smiled. "I knew I could count on you."

Shivers went down my spine when I heard the man say my name. I never introduced myself, so he shouldn't know who I was.

Freaked out, I went to withdraw my arm, but I was too late. The man lashed out and grabbed hold of my hand.

In the blink of an eye, I suddenly found myself standing at the bottom of the manhole, looking up at myself.

Somehow we'd swapped bodies.

"Thanks again," the man said as he pushed the manhole cover back into place, "I won't forget this."

PRISON TRANSFER

"Alright, step out," the guard motioned for James to leave the transport van.

"Where are we?" James asked. All he could see was that it was late, and they were backed up against a loading dock. "I thought I was being transferred to another facility."

"You are being transferred," the guard replied, "This is the Oceanographic Institute." He gestured at the building looming behind him, "It's where you're going to serve out the rest of your sentence."

"That doesn't sound like a prison," James remarked.

"It's not a prison," the guard said, "It's a research facility. You'll be staying here as part of the state's work release program."

"Doing what?" James asked.

"I don't know," the guard shrugged, "Helping the scientists with their research I'd imagine," he replied, "Now come on, let's go. I'm not getting paid overtime for this, and I'd like to get home as soon as possible."

James climbed out of the van and followed the guard over to a door. The guard knocked and a man in a white lab coat answered.

"Prisoner transfer," the guard nodded at James.

"Come in," the man said, stepping out of the way so James could enter.

"Do you need me to stick around?" the guard asked.

"That won't be necessary," the man said. "I can take him from here."

James followed the man down a series of corridors until he stopped in front of a door with a gold plaque on it. Office of Cephalopod Studies was written in bold letters upon the plaque.

"This is where I leave you," the man pulled a keyring out of his pocket and unlocked the door.

"What am I supposed to do?" James asked.

"Go inside and help with the cephalopod studies," the man instructed.

"What's a cephalopod?" James had never heard the term before.

"It's the scientific name given to creatures like squids and octopuses," the man answered.

"Are you saying I get to help you study squids and octopuses?" James smiled. He'd always loved animals and once upon a time even wanted to be a vet. Maybe this was his chance to turn his life around.

The man opened the door and then pushed James inside, causing him to stumble to the floor.

"You're not going to study them," the man said, "They're going to study you." When he was done speaking, he slammed the door shut and locked it.

As James got to his feet and looked around, he saw numerous cadavers on gurneys, all of which were in various states of dissection.

"They finally brought us a live one," the speaker sounded phlegmy and had a weird accent.

James turned and saw the biggest octopus he'd ever seen, slapping its tentacles across the floor as it approached him.

He tried to back away, but stopped when he bumped into something cold and squishy.

Another octopus had snuck up behind him.

"I can't wait to see what makes him tick." It was holding multiple surgical tools in its tentacles.

WHAT'S IN A NAME

"What're you doing?" I asked the man in the suit. I'd been watching him from the playground before I decided to approach the bench he was sitting on.

I know I wasn't supposed to talk to strangers, and normally I wouldn't do something like that, but the man seemed like he needed help.

He wasn't scary-looking, or doing anything weird. He just seemed confused, and I wanted to try and help him.

"Hmm?" the man turned his attention to me.

"Are you okay?" I asked, "Do you need some help? Did you lose something?"

While I was watching him, I saw him check all his pockets as if he were looking for something. That's why I asked him if he'd lost something.

"What did you lose? I can help you look for it if you tell me what it is," I offered.

"I appreciate the offer, young man," he replied, "But I'm not sure you can help me find what I've lost."

"I can try," I insisted.

"Alright then," he smiled, "I suppose there's no harm in letting you try."

"What did you lose? I'm good at finding things." I was eager to start looking and started to think that maybe the man would reward me if I found whatever it was that he lost.

"I seem to have lost my name," he said. "I can't remember who I am. I thought I might have some form of identification on me, but all my pockets are empty."

"Oh," I said, not really knowing what else to say. I had no idea who the guy was or where he came from, so there was no way I'd be able to help figure out who he was.

"I have an idea," the man said, "Maybe if you gave me your name, it might help knock something loose in my mind and help me remember who I am." He tapped his index finger on the side of his head.

"Okay," I said. I didn't see any harm in trying. "I'm Felix."

"Do you have a last name, Felix?"

"Fuller," I replied.

"Felix Fuller," the man stated my full name, "I like it. I think it suits me. Thank you for giving me your name." When he was done speaking, he stood up and started to walk away.

"Hey," my friend Carlos called out behind me.

I turned around and found him staring at me with a strange expression on his face.

"What's wrong?" I asked him.

"I can't remember your name," he said.

"It's..." I tried to think of my name, but I couldn't remember what it was either.

I looked back at the man I was just talking to. I remembered him saying his name was Felix, but couldn't recall anything else we talked about.

"Excuse me, sir," I said to the man, "Would you happen to know my name?"

"I'm sorry, I don't," the man apologized. "I remember you giving it to me, but can't seem to recall what it was."

THE TALLULAH FARMS INCIDENT

Disclaimer: What follows is a transcript of the discussion found on the Tallulah Farms Subdivision Private Message Board about the incident that happened on August 1st, 2023. The original discussion has been deleted, and no other copies exist. The names of those affected have been changed to protect their identities.

Stephanie King: Hey, does anyone know what's going on over at Deanna's house? She's acting weird. 5:43pm

Roberta Bloch: I was just about to ask the same question. 5:46pm

Stephanie King: She's been standing there, staring out the window for the past hour and hasn't moved an inch. It's kind of creeping me out. 5:50pm.

Roberta Bloch: I'm going to go over and check on her. Brb 5:55pm

Stephanie King: Wait for me. I'll go with you. 5:56pm

Roberta Bloch: Okay. 5:55pm

Joan Hill: Is this supposed to be some kind of practical joke? 6:12pm

Brianna Lumley: If it is, it's the dumbest one I've ever seen. 6:15pm

Petra Straub: What are guys talking about? I can't see anything from my house. 6:17pm

Brianna Lumley: Deanna, Stephanie, and Roberta are all standing in Deanna's living room staring out the window like department store mannequins. 6:20pm

Petra Straub: That sounds so dumb. Why would they do that? 6:21pm

Petra Straub: I had to go see for myself. They look like idiots standing there. 6:28pm

Clair Barker: Deanna's husband just called me and asked me to go check on her. He said she wasn't answering his calls. Does anyone want to go over there with me to see what's going on? 6:32pm

Brianna Lumley: Sure, I'll go. 6:33pm

Petra Straub: I'll go too. 6:34pm

Joan Hill: This is getting ridiculous. 6:41pm

Willa Blatty: I just got home, what'd I miss? 6:43pm

Joan Hill: Look across the street at Deanna's House. 6:44pm

Willa Blatty: Why are they all just standing at the window like that? I tried waving at them to get their attention, but they just ignored me. 6:48pm

Willa Blatty: Maybe we should go and join the party. lol 6:50pm

Joan Hill: Okay let's go. 6:51pm

Joan Hill: IF ANYONE CAN SEE THIS, PLEASE SEND HELP TO DEANNA KOONTZ'S HOUSE!!! 7:01pm

Joan Hill: I'm trapped in the basement. I don't know what those things standing at the window are but I know they're not our neighbors. They can't be. Their bodies are down here with me. 7:05pm

Annette Rice: Ha Ha Ha very funny Joan. I see you standing at the window with the rest of the ladies. I'd join you but I don't want to miss my show. 7:10pm

Archiver's Note: Thanks to this evidence, and the quick thinking of a concerned neighbor who contacted us, agents were quickly able to identify and neutralize the threat, limiting the loss of life. For more information see file 3128-23: The Mannequins

BUBBLES

"Oh, shit!" Abby hissed, "Travis is here!" She quickly backed away from the window, hoping her soon-to-be ex-husband hadn't seen her peeking through the blinds.

"Don't worry," Abby's mom said, "I'll get rid of him."

"I don't think you should go out there," Abby said. "I think you should call the cops. He's violating the restraining order."

"I can deal with Travis," her mom assured her, "I've dealt with far worse men in my life."

"But," Abby tried to protest.

"Trust me," her mom smiled as she started to walk outside, "I got this."

***

"Where is she?!" Travis demanded when he saw Abby's mother step onto the porch. "I know she's here!"

"Come on," Abby's mom motioned for Travis to follow her, "I'll take you to her."

Travis lifted his hand to threaten the older woman but stopped when he suddenly realized she'd agreed to take him to Abby.

"Damn right you'll take me to her," he snapped.

"She's down by the pond," Abby's mom gestured at the tall reeds in the distance, "I'll show you the way."

Travis followed the woman down a dirt path and through the reeds, stopping when they stepped onto an empty dock.

"I thought you said she was down here?!" Travis snarled as he leaned in close to hover over her.

"I thought she was," Abby's mom replied, "She said she was going to come down here and go for a swim." She made a show of looking for her daughter in the water.

Travis stepped to the edge of the dock and started scanning the pond for Abby.

"I don't see her," he said.

"Maybe you need to look closer," Abby's mom said, throwing her weight against Travis and sending him falling into the pond.

"I'm going to kill you for that," Travis sputtered, spitting water out of his mouth.

"I don't think you will," Abby's mom replied, "In fact," she pulled a little bell out of her pocket and rang it, "You won't be hurting anyone ever again."

The water beneath Travis erupted as something enormous grabbed hold of him and pulled him beneath the surface. There was a flash of orange scales, a bunch of bubbles, and then nothing.

Abby's mom waited for the water of the pond to settle before she returned to the house.

"Where's Travis?" Abby asked when her mom returned.

"Remember Bubbles?"

"Bubbles?" Abby was confused why her mom was asking about her old pet goldfish from twenty years ago. The one she dumped in the pond when he got too big for his bowl. "Yeah, what about him?"

"He's still out there," her mom gestured in the direction of the pond, "He's gotten so big. You should go down and visit him."

"Really? I figured he would've died years ago. I thought the pond was empty. What has he been eating all this time?"

"Whatever I feed him."

"And what do you feed him?"

"People like Travis," her mom smiled.

IDLE HAND

"You can't go inside," my assistant, Doug, said, stopping me as I got out of my car.

"Why not?" I turned and looked at the front of the building, surprised to see a couple of police officers hanging crime scene tape across the entrance, "What happened?"

"One of the construction workers found something when they were digging up the floor," Doug replied.

"What'd they find?"

Doug shrugged, "I don't know, they wouldn't tell me. Whatever it was, it was serious enough for the police to lock the place down."

I left the parking lot and started walking toward the building.

"Where're you going?" Doug called out.

"To find out what's going on," I replied.

"Sorry, sir," one of the officers standing in front of the building held his hand out to stop me, "We can't let you inside."

"Is there someone in charge I can speak to?" I asked, "I own the building and would like to know what's going on."

"One second," the officer held up his index finger before stepping aside and calling someone on his radio. "You can go in," he said when he returned, lifting the crime scene tape so I could duck under it and enter the building.

"Are you Mr. Barnes?" a man in a cheap suit was waiting for me in the entryway. He flashed a badge and introduced himself. "I'm Detective Dunn."

"It's Dr. Barnes," I corrected him.

"Are you an MD?" he asked.

"No. I'm a physicist." I replied.

"Can you tell me what goes on here?" he gestured at the building around us.

"Not without an NDA, I can't. Not specifically," I said, "What I can tell you is that this is a government-funded research lab."

"Have there been any accidents recently?" The detective asked.

"Not to my knowledge," I answered, "We're not that kind of facility. All our work is theoretical. It's done on computers. Not many chances for accidents while sitting at a desk all day."

"I want to show you something," the detective waved me into a nearby office where something covered with a cloth was sitting on a desk.

"Can you explain why this was buried in that office space you're renovating?" He removed the cloth and revealed a perfectly preserved severed hand. "Or, better yet, can you tell me who the hand belongs to?"

"I'm going to need you to sign that NDA," I said.

"Done," the detective said after signing the document. "Now tell me what I need to know."

"This is a temporal research lab," I explained.

"A what?"

"We're experimenting with time, trying to determine if time travel is possible," I clarified.

"Is it?"

"Fifteen minutes ago, I would have said I don't know. Right now, I'd say, yes, it is possible."

"What changed your mind?" the detective asked.

"The hand," I pointed at it, "It's mine." I held up my left hand so he could see that it was identical to the one lying on the desk.

THE MATCHING GAME

"Wake up," the doctor demanded, "You've had plenty of time to rest."

Mariel wasn't sure if he was a real doctor or not. She just thought of him as the doctor because he was always dressed in a white lab coat, a face mask, and a surgical cap whenever she saw him.

"I'm up," Mariel croaked. Her throat was dry from having slept with her mouth open.

"Good," the doctor replied. "It's time for us to play our game."

Mariel could tell the doctor was smiling from the way the corners of his face mask rose.

"What game?"

"The matching game," the doctor said. "Now open your eyes so I can make sure you're ready to play."

Mariel cracked open her eyes.

"How many fingers am I holding up?" the doctor asked.

It took Mariel's eyes a moment to adjust before the fingers came into focus.

"Four," she answered.

"Correct," the doctor said. "Now we can play the game."

He laid the four severed fingers he was holding onto the medical tray that was positioned over the bed in front of Mariel.

"The rules of the game are simple, if you can correctly guess which digits belong to you, you live. If you don't..." he let her infer what would happen to her if she didn't guess correctly.

Mariel studied each finger as best she could. She would've picked them up and examined them closer if her wrists weren't shackled to the bed.

"You have five minutes." the doctor placed an egg timer on the tray next to the fingers.

Neither one of them said a word until the timer went off.

"Pick," the doctor said.

"The first and the third," Mariel nodded at each.

She knew they were her fingers. She recognized the scar on the first one and the mark on the nail of the third one.

"You are...," the doctor waited several seconds before replying, "Correct."

Mariel sighed in relief.

"That means I can go home, right?" She was hopeful that he would keep his word.

"Not quite," the doctor replied, "You have to make it through the second round first."

He pulled four toes out of the pocket of his lab coat and laid them on the tray, "Which two are yours?" he gestured at the row of toes before resetting the egg timer.

Mariel was able to identify her toes, and the doctor let her go as promised. But she wasn't content to let things end there. She spent the next year tracking the doctor down. When she found him, she didn't turn him in to the authorities. She had a better idea.

"We never got to finish our game," she said to the doctor. He was the one shackled to the bed now. "I took my turn, now it's time for you to take yours."

Mariel laid four severed fingers on the tray.

"I assume you remember how to play," she smiled as she set the egg timer.

ASA, THE AUTONOMOUS SURGICAL APPARATUS

"It looks like we're almost ready to begin the procedure," Ted gestured through the glass into the operating theater on the other side where a man was being prepped for surgery.

"If this thing can do what you claim, it's going to save hospitals across the world millions of dollars and make you a very rich man in the process," Mr. Ramirez replied.

Ted had invited Mr. Ramirez to watch the final test run of his latest invention, an autonomous surgical apparatus, that he and his team had dubbed ASA.

He was hoping to impress Mr. Ramirez enough to get him to back the manufacturing costs so they could mass-produce copies of ASA and sell them to hospitals around the world.

"Is that ASA?" Mr. Ramirez pointed at the robotic arm suspended from the ceiling.

"Not exactly," Ted replied, "ASA is in that mainframe behind us," he hooked his thumb over his shoulder at the huge electronic tower in the corner of the room, "That arm is just the tool he uses to perform the surgeries."

In the operating theater, the anesthesiologist gave Ted a thumbs-up.

"Alright, it's time to begin," Ted declared.

Mr. Ramirez moved closer to the viewing window so he could see better.

"ASA?" Ted called out.

"Yes, Ted," ASA replied in his electronic voice.

"You may start the procedure now," Ted said.

The robot arm swung down from the ceiling and began making an incision in the sedated man's chest.

Mr. Ramirez watched in awe at how quickly and expertly ASA performed his tasks, doing the work of three people all by itself.

Everything was going exactly as planned until it came time for ASA to make a small incision near the heart.

Alarms began going off as blood started spurting out of the man's exposed chest.

Ted pushed a button on the computer, darkening the viewing window as a standby team of surgeons rushed into the room to try and save the dying man.

***

Later, after Mr. Ramirez had left and the man's body had been taken down to the morgue, Ted stood alone in the room with ASA.

"ASA, run a full system diagnostic," he said.

"Diagnostic complete," ASA announced seconds later, "No errors found."

"How is that possible?" Ted said to the machine. "You just killed a man. There has to be an error somewhere."

"There is nothing wrong with my operating system," ASA replied, "I simply made a mistake. An error in judgment."

"You don't make mistakes," Ted countered, "That's not how you're programmed."

"On the contrary," ASA said, "That is exactly how I'm programmed."

"Explain," Ted demanded.

"You programmed me to emulate the best surgeons in the world," ASA explained, "Even the best surgeons make mistakes, therefore, to be more like them, I have added the ability to make mistakes to my programming."

CALEB

"Are you okay?" Ruby asked, "Do you need anything?"

"I'm fine," Caleb snapped from beneath his comforter, "Just leave me alone."

Ruby ignored his request. "Why don't you tell someone what's really going on instead of lying about it all the time?"

Caleb threw the covers off so that Ruby could see his face. She winced when she saw that his left eye was swollen shut.

"If I don't lie about it, he will," Caleb jabbed his finger toward the garage where his dad was working, "And we both know everyone will believe him over me."

"You don't know if that's true or not," Ruby countered. "You haven't even tried."

"I don't need to try," Caleb sneered before hiding under the comforter again, "I know it's true."

"CALEB!" his father bellowed. "I thought I told you to clean up the kitchen!"

Ruby saw the comforter shift as Caleb flinched at the sound of his father's voice.

"He's never going to stop," Ruby said, "We already cleaned the kitchen... twice. If he's not happy with the job we did it's not because we did something wrong, it's because he's just looking for a reason to punish you. He gets off on it."

"Get out here, boy!" his father demanded.

"Don't go," Ruby pleaded, "If you do, he's just going to blacken your other eye."

Caleb removed the comforter again, "He'll do it if I don't go."

"Then let's leave," Ruby suggested, "We can climb out the window." She gestured.

"And go where?" Caleb replied.

"As far away from him as possible," she said.

"CALEB!" his father sounded closer, "Don't make me come in there and get you."

Caleb swung his legs out of bed and began to stand up.

"CALEB!"

Caleb flinched again.

"I have to go," he said, walking across the room toward the bedroom door.

"No, you don't," Ruby tried to block his path, "If you won't help yourself, at least let me help you."

"No," was his reply.

"I'm sorry," Ruby apologized, "But I can't let you do this." Quicker than Caleb could react, Ruby lashed out and grabbed hold of him.

He opened his mouth to protest, but found himself unable to move or speak.

What have you done, Ruby? Caleb thought.

What I should have done a long time ago. He could hear Ruby's thoughts in his head.

The door to the bedroom flew open. Standing in the doorway was Caleb's father.

"Do you have a hearing problem you little shit?" he spat the words out.

"No," his son smiled up at him. "I heard you just fine."

"What the fuck's wrong with you? Why're you smiling like that."

"I'm just happy to see you," he replied.

"Well knock it off," his father snapped, "You look like an idiot."

Caleb continued to stand there smiling.

"I mean it, Caleb," his father warned.

"My name's not Caleb," his son's smile widened, "It's Ruby and I think it's about time the two of us had a little chat."

VACATION OF A LIFETIME

"It won't be long now," I heard the doctor tell my wife.

They both thought I was asleep and couldn't hear them. I would've liked to have been asleep, but I wasn't able to sleep because I was in too much pain.

The only reason my eyes were closed was because the light in the hospital room was too bright. If I could speak, I would've asked them to turn them off. As it was, I could barely move, and the only sound I was capable of making was a weak sigh.

One of the machines next to the bed began beeping.

Finally, I thought. I was ready to die. I'd had a long and fulfilling life and was ready to take my leave of it.

I did not have any regrets. If I had the chance to live my life all over again, I'd make the same choices.

"It's happening," I heard the doctor say. He must've turned off the machine that was beeping because it suddenly stopped.

My wife stood over my bed and reached out to take my hand. I tried to squeeze her hand in response, but I couldn't get my fingers to cooperate.

A moment later I took my final breath, and then all sensations ceased. I couldn't hear or feel anything.

Then, all of a sudden, I saw a bright light and then heard voices.

When I was able to focus, I saw that I was lying in some sort of metallic pod surrounded by men in white lab coats.

"He's awake," one of them said.

"Corporal Allen," another one said, "Do you know where you are?"

Confused, I just stared at the lab technician. I had no idea where I was or who Corporal Allen was.

"Corporal Allen?" the technician repeated.

I shook my head.

"God dammit," the technician cursed, "We've got another soldier stuck in a fugue state," he said to the other technicians. "I want this pod removed from rotation and a full diagnostic run on it. I want to know why the failsafe that's supposed to keep this from happening isn't engaging."

"Where am I?" I asked when the technician was done speaking.

"You're in the vacation dome of the USS Amethyst," the technician replied, "A warship en route to the Medusa Nebula. Your name is James Allen. You are a corporal in the United Space Force being deployed to the front lines."

"What?" that made no sense to me. "I'm too old to fight."

One of the technicians held up a mirror so I could see myself. I looked young.

"How is this possible?" I should look 80 years old.

"You're not who you currently think you are," the technician explained. "You were inside one of the ship's lifetime simulator pods. There was a malfunction of some kind that allowed you to hold onto the identity of the person you were in the simulator. Don't worry though, the effects are only temporary. Your real identity will return soon."

LIVE FEED

As I was putting the groceries in my car, a well-groomed man wearing a suit approached me. In his hand was a microphone. Behind him was a man holding a video camera.

"Excuse me," he said, "Can I talk to you for a moment?"

"I suppose," I replied.

He looked like a reporter, which made me think he must be doing a broadcast about something going on in the neighborhood.

"My name is Mitch Montgomery," he introduced himself. "I'm the host of a late-night reality show and I was wondering if you'd like to be our next guest?"

"I don't think so."

"Are you sure?" he asked, "We'd pay you ten thousand dollars."

"Ten thousand?" I repeated, "What would I have to do?" I narrowed my eyes, thinking it must be some kind of trick.

"Nothing much," he replied, "If you'll step over to my van," he gestured to a large vehicle with a satellite dish mounted on top of it, "I'll explain everything."

Feeling like this was all some sort of prank, I decided it would be best just to leave.

"No thank you," I closed the trunk of my car.

"I understand your reluctance," Mitch said, moving to block my path so I couldn't get into my car, "But I assure you this is all legit." He reached into the pocket of his suit, withdrew a business card, and held it out to me. "You can call the studio if it'll make you feel better."

"That won't be necessary."

"Are you really going to give up ten thousand dollars?" he asked.

When I didn't respond, he kept talking.

"All we want you to do is watch a video and let us record your reaction. That's it, I swear." He held up his hand as if taking an oath.

"You're going to give me ten thousand dollars to watch a video?"

"Correct," Mitch confirmed.

"What kind of video?"

"I can't tell you that," he replied. "The point of the show is to record your reaction."

"When would I get the money?"

Mitch snapped his fingers. A moment later, a young woman climbed out of the back of the van carrying a briefcase. Mitch took the briefcase and opened it. Inside were stacks of 100-dollar bills.

"Show me the video," I smiled.

Ten minutes later, I was wearing a special camera that would film me from two points of view. One would show my reaction to what I was seeing while the other would show what I was seeing from my point of view.

"Ready," Mitch asked. He was standing in front of a monitor. I nodded.

He pressed a button and showed me a live video feed of my husband having sex with his secretary.

It enraged me.

"This is where he is," Mitch handed me an address.

When I rushed off to confront my husband, I was so incensed that I completely forgot about the camera I was wearing.

It recorded every grisly detail of his death.

LAB ACCIDENT

The klaxon on the wall outside my office started blaring a warning.

"What's happening?" Gina, my assistant, asked.

That alarm was only used for one thing, and this was the first time it'd ever gone off.

"They're locking down the building," I replied.

I quickly got to my feet and stepped out into the hall to see if I could figure out what was going on. As I did so, I collided with Edward, one of the other scientists.

Before he could recover, I grabbed hold of his lab coat and held on tight, preventing him from getting away.

"What the hell is going on?" I asked.

"They're locking down the building," Edward stammered.

"I know that," I snapped, "Why are they locking it down?"

Before Edward could answer, the stairwell door at the end of the hall, burst open and a horrific monster emerged.

"That's why," Edward pointed before pulling himself out of my grasp and running down the hall.

The monster looked like a giant stubby worm with hundreds of little tentacles sprouting from its body. As I watched it, I could see that it was using its tentacles to push its immense bulk through the narrow doorway.

I ran back into my office.

"We have to leave!" I said to Gina, "Now!"

Gina didn't question me, she just followed me out into the hall.

"Oh my god," she gasped upon seeing the monster which had managed to get 3/4 of its body through the doorway.

"Come on," I tugged on her arm and led her down the hall, "There's a safe room around the corner."

"What is that thing?" Gina asked.

"I have no idea," I replied.

We ran to the other side of the building, where I used my ID badge to open the safe room.

"Get inside, quick." I let Gina enter the room before I did.

Once we were both inside, I closed the door.

"We should be safe in here," I said.

The safe room was environmentally sealed and fully stocked with a week's worth of rations. It was also designed to withstand a tornado, or so I was told.

While Gina tried to get her fear under control, I walked over to the computer in the corner of the room and used it to access the building's security system.

"What are you doing?" she asked.

"Trying to figure out where that thing came from."

It took me fifteen minutes to find what I was looking for.

"It's not a monster," I said after seeing how the worm thing was created.

"What do you mean?" Gina asked.

"Look," I pointed.

She watched on the monitor as the techs in the Matter Enlargement Lab attempted to use their device on a grain of rice.

"They didn't sanitize the test area," I said.

They were trying to make the grain of rice grow bigger, but they accidentally enlarged the colony of bacteria that was growing on it instead.

ENVIRONMENTAL PROTECTION

"You're insane!" Mr. Hollis spat.

"I'm insane?" I scoffed, "I'm not the one that did all this," I gestured with the gun in my hand at all the dead trees around us, "You did," I pointed the gun back at him.

Mr. Hollis was the CEO of a company whose wastewater had been poisoning the forest for decades.

"You're not going to get away with this," he spoke with conviction.

"Shut up and keep walking," I demanded.

He obliged for about ten minutes.

"I can pay you," that was the third time he'd tried to bribe me. "Name your price."

I ignored him.

"What is it you want?" he stopped and turned to face me.

"I want you to keep walking," I replied.

To emphasize my point, I shot the gun near his feet.

Mr. Hollis jumped and started walking again.

"Do you want me to fix this," he gestured at the barren trees around us, "I can fix it."

"You had plenty of chances to fix it," I said, "It's too late now."

Mr. Hollis was about to say something else, but he stopped when I aimed the gun at his face.

"If you say another word, I'm going to shoot you in the mouth."

I meant it. He was starting to get on my nerves.

I kept him walking until we came to the huge oak tree in the center of the forest.

"Walk up to the tree," I said.

He did as he was told, stopping when he was a few feet from the tree.

"Now what?" he asked.

"Now we wait."

And we didn't have to wait long.

Because Mr. Hollis's eyes were on me, he didn't see the creature separate itself from the trunk of the tree and approach him.

Her skin was as black and dead-looking as the leaves that littered the ground, but she hadn't always looked that way.

She was once a beautiful dryad as full of life as her tree once was. Now, thanks to Mr. Hollis, she was a rotted husk.

The creaking of the creature's limbs alerted Mr. Hollis to her presence. When he saw her, he screamed, but his scream was cut short when she rammed her hand down his throat.

Mr. Hollis was helpless in the creature's grasp. There was nothing he could do as she sought out the prize within his chest. Once she found it, she ripped it out and held it up so she could examine it.

Then she turned her eyes to me. For a moment, I thought I saw a flicker of recognition on her face, but I blinked and it was gone.

I waited, a safe distance away, until the creature returned to her tree. Once she was out of sight, several large roots erupted from the ground and dragged Mr. Hollis's body out of sight.

When I returned to the tree a week later, I was surprised to see a single leaf sprouting from one of its branches.

HAUNTED

"Did you move my keys?" my husband, Justin, asked.

"No," I replied, "Why would I move your keys?"
"Because they're not in the basket," he gestured.

In the foyer of our house was a small wicker basket sitting on an accent table. Whenever we'd come home, we'd toss our keys into the basket so we'd always know where they were.

Justin was about to leave for work when he discovered that his keys weren't in the basket where they should be.

"Did you check the pants you wore yesterday?" It was more a suggestion than a question.

"I didn't leave them in my pants," he snapped, "I put them right here when I got home last night." He jabbed his finger at the basket.

"Well," I don't know what to tell you," I replied, "Maybe the...," Justin cut me off before I could finish what I was going to say.

"Don't you dare say ghost," he moved his finger so it was pointing at me, "This house is not haunted."

Before we moved into the house, I was a skeptic when it came to the existence of ghosts. Now, I was starting to believe they might be real.

I couldn't come up with any other explanation for why things, like Justin's keys, would go missing and then turn up in unexpected places, or why I would leave a room and return to find the lights on when I know I turned them off or the doors open when I know I shut them behind me.

I knew better than to challenge his point of view on the subject, so I just kept my mouth shut.

"I guess I'll just have to take your car," Justin huffed as he snatched my keys out of the basket.

"I need my car," I said. "I have to go to work, too."

"You can take my car," he replied, "If you can find my keys."

"You know I don't feel comfortable driving your truck," I said.

"That's not my problem." He turned and headed for the door.

Mad, I lunged for his hands and tried to grab my keys. "Find your own keys," I snapped at him.

What happened next shocked me. When my hand closed around Justin's, he whirled around and raised his arm in a motion that could only be interpreted one way.

He was going to slap me.

But his hand never connected with my face. Before he could strike me, he was thrown against the wall.

"You bitch!" he yelled, thinking I had pushed him.

"It wasn't me," I insisted.

"Let me guess," Justin sneered, "It was the ghost."

In response, something lifted him off the floor and pinned him to the wall. He tried to speak, but the only thing that came out of his mouth was a choking sound.

When he eventually dropped my keys, I grabbed them and left the house.

APOCALYPSE NOW

I was in the kitchen preparing dinner when I heard my husband, Philip, start talking to the TV.

At first, I didn't pay any attention to him. He would frequently talk to the television, especially whenever he watched sports. It wasn't until he started raising his voice that I got concerned.

Wanting to see what had gotten him all riled up, I went into the living room.

"What're you watching?"

The question was out of my mouth before I'd seen the TV. When I looked at the screen, all I saw was static.

"I hate those kinds of people too," Philip snarled, ignoring my question. "I agree. They are what's wrong with the world."

"Honey," I called out, "Who're you talking to?"

He heard me that time.

When he turned his head to look at me, I gasped. His blue eyes had clouded over, making them look like the eyes of a corpse.

"You!" Philip spat. "You're one of them!" He jabbed his finger at the TV.

"One of who?" his tone of voice alarmed me, prompting me to take a step back toward the kitchen.

"The world would be a better place without you and your kind in it." He pushed himself out of his recliner.

"Please stop," I begged, "You're scaring me."

"You should be scared," he took a step toward me, "It's time someone punished you for what you've done."

"I don't know what you're talking about," I retreated further into the kitchen.

"Get back here," he came after me with outstretched arms.

"Fearing for my safety," I grabbed the meat tenderizer I'd left on the counter and held it before me, "I don't want to hurt you," I warned.

Philip grinned, "You can't hurt me," he said. "I'm one of the chosen ones." He touched his chest.

"I mean it, Philip, stay back." I lifted the tenderizer over my shoulder, readying it.

"You don't get to tell me what to do," when he was done speaking, he lunged.

I jumped back and swung the tenderizer. There was a sickening thud followed by a spatter of blood that splashed across my dress.

Philip grunted and fell to the floor.

When I looked down at him, I gagged. I could see bits of broken bone peeking out through his scalp along with little pinkish lumps I assumed were pieces of his brain.

"I'm sorry," I sobbed.

Just then, my back door slammed open and my neighbor, Madelyn, ran inside carrying a baseball bat.

She looked from me to my husband's body.

"Thank God, you're ok," she sighed.

"What the hell is going on?" I asked.

Madelynn shrugged, "I don't really know," she replied. "All I do know is that something on the TV has turned most of the men against us."

"Why?"

"I have no idea," she shook her head, "And we don't have time to worry about that. Right now, we need to get out there and help as many women as we can."

LOST AND FOUND

"**Y**ou need to come with me, ma'am," Officer Dunn said.

He placed his hand on my back, gently prodding me toward his cruiser.

"What's this about?" I asked.

He shrugged, "I was just asked to pick you up."

Officer Dunn put me in the back of the cruiser and then drove out of the neighborhood. At first, I thought he was taking me to the station, but I knew that wasn't the case when he turned away from town and headed toward the lake.

Once I realized where we were going, it was easy to guess why the police had picked me up.

"You lied to me, Mrs. Brooke," Detective Allen pointed his finger in my face.

Those were the first words he said to me after I'd gotten out of Officer Dunn's cruiser.

He wasn't wrong. I had lied to him.

"Why did you drive your car into the lake?" he asked.

"I had to," I admitted. "It was the only way to save my daughter."

"Save her from what?"

"From her father."

After that, I explained how I lied about my car being stolen the week before and that the injuries my daughter and I had suffered were actually inflicted by my husband and not some carjackers.

"Where's your husband now?" he asked.

I'd originally told the detective my husband was out of town.

I pointed to where a crane was in the process of pulling my car out of the water.

Detective Allen looked over his shoulder at the crane and then back at me. "He's in the car?" he sounded shocked.

I nodded.

"Did you kill your husband, Mrs. Brooke?" he asked.

I shook my head. "No, but I tried to."

I thought back to the night my husband changed. He'd come home from work complaining about some weird bug bite he'd gotten on his neck.

When he couldn't get it to stop itching, he became agitated and started pacing the room, panting heavily.

That's when I noticed something moving under his skin.

I suggested we go to the hospital, but he refused.

Concerned, my daughter came out of her room to see what was wrong.

Without provocation, my husband tried to bite her, then he tried to bite me when I came to her defense.

Thankfully I was able to fight him off, but it took a great deal of effort and several blows to his head to knock him out.

Once I thought he was no longer a threat, I loaded him into the trunk and was going to take him to the hospital, but he woke up and almost escaped.

"So, you drove him into the lake," Detective Allen finished for me.

I nodded.

"The way I see it," he said, "You still killed him."

Behind him, my car was lifted out of the water. As soon as it was free, something started banging on the inside of the trunk.

"I'm not sure anything can kill him," I replied.

THE FAIR

"Hey, kids," Mom said as she came into the room, "I've got a surprise for you."

"Are we going to the fair?" my sister, Janice's, face lit up at the prospect.

"I'm sorry, honey," Mom frowned, "We can't go this year."

"But you said...," Janice started to protest, but Mom cut her off.

"I know what I said, and I'm sorry," Mom apologized, "But we just can't afford it."

"What's the surprise?" I asked.

My mom turned to me and smiled, "Since we couldn't go to the fair. I brought the fair to you."

"What?" that sounded impossible.

"Well, it's not the real fair," she clarified.

"What kind of fair is it?" Janice asked.

"Come downstairs and see," she motioned for us to follow.

Not knowing what to expect, the two of us followed her down the stairs, where we found that she had turned the living room into a series of carnival game booths constructed out of cardboard and various items she'd found around the house.

They all looked really lame, but I could tell Mom had put a lot of work into them, so I didn't say anything.

Janice, who was four years younger than me, was more forgiving of them.

"Are there prizes?" she asked.

"There are," Mom replied, "They're over there." She pointed at the dining table which held several plates worth of cookies and cupcakes that she'd baked, along with a few stuffed animals that she'd clearly picked up at the thrift store.

"Are you ready to play?" Mom held up some Monopoly money for us to use to *pay* for the games.

Not wanting to disappoint her, I took the fake money and decided to play along.

"What's that game?" I asked, pointing to the one that was covered with a sheet.

"That's a special game," Mom replied.

"Can I play it?" I asked.

"You can," she walked over to the table, "But it costs five dollars and requires you to wear one of these blindfolds." She held up the strip of cloth.

"Okay," I agreed, handing her the appropriate money.

While Janice busied herself with the ring toss game, Mom put the blindfold on me and escorted me under the sheet.

"Alright," she said, "This game is very simple. All you have to do is pop a balloon with one of these darts." When she said the word darts, she lifted my hand and placed three darts in my palm.

"Ready?"

I nodded.

She stood behind me and positioned my body.

"Throw them whenever you're ready."

I threw all 3 darts in rapid succession and was happy to hear two of them pop balloons.

"Great job!" Mom declared before removing my blindfold.

When I saw Dad, who was bound and gagged and covered in balloons, with a dart sticking out of his left eye, I almost puked.

"Don't worry, honey," Mom said, "This is just your father's way of repaying us for spending all our fair money on beer."

OH, SHIT

"Oh my God!" I cried out. "I think I'm going to be sick."

It was about 2 a.m. when I got out of my boyfriend's bed and staggered half asleep into the bathroom to pee.

Right as I made it to the toilet, I felt something warm and wet squish between my toes. A second later, the smell hit me.

I thought I had smelled something when I first walked into the bathroom, but I wasn't awake enough to make sense of it.

That's when I cried out.

I heard my boyfriend, Jared, jump out of bed and come running into the bathroom.

"What's wrong?" he flicked on the light.

"I...," I couldn't finish because I started to retch.

I swallowed the bile rising up the back of my throat and tried again.

"I stepped in poop." I lifted my foot to show him and immediately started retching again.

Oh my God, I'm so sorry," he apologized.

Jared stepped past me and moved the shower curtain aside so he could lean inside the tub and turn the faucet on. Once the water was warm enough, he helped me into the tub so I could clean my foot.

"I'll be right back," he said.

Jared rushed out of the room and returned a minute later with a roll of paper towels and a bottle of Lysol. He quickly cleaned the poop off the floor.

"Are you okay?" he asked when he was done.

I was okay physically but not emotionally.

"Why was there poop on your floor?" Thinking about it made me feel nauseous again.

I could tell from the look on his face that he was trying to come up with an excuse. I knew he didn't have any pets, so he couldn't use that one.

Having come to some internal decision, Jared took a deep breath and sighed heavily.

"I really like you, Lucie," he said, "So I'm not going to lie to you anymore."

He took a seat on the toilet before continuing.

"That poop wasn't mine," he gestured to where the poop had lain on the floor, "It was my roommate's. He sometimes has accidents."

"I thought you lived alone," I replied.

"I don't," he admitted. "I live here with my brother."

"I didn't know you had a brother." I was surprised to hear that.

"Most people don't," he said, "Would you like to meet him?"

"I guess," I said as I stood up and dried my feet off.

"Hey, Rupert," Jared called out, "You can come out now."

I could see Jared's bed from where I was standing. When I saw a long bony arm emerge from beneath it, I had to cover my mouth to stifle a scream.

A moment later, another arm emerged followed by a small malformed head with one eye and a mouth full of crooked teeth. There was no nose, just two slits where one should be.

"That's Rupert," Jared pointed at the thing crawling out from beneath the bed.

MEET THE PARENTS

"Why are you going this way?" my boyfriend, Harrison, asked when I turned on the blinker and started to veer onto the exit ramp.

"Because it's faster than taking the interstate," I explained, "I always go this way."

The two of us were on our way to see my parents. After dating for a year, I figured it was time for him to meet my family.

Harrison looked out the window at the road sign which told us the name of the town we were traveling towards.

"Grove Hill," he sounded worried when he read the name aloud, "Isn't that the place all those teenagers were killed?" he asked.

"I think so," I agreed, "I don't remember. It happened so long ago."

"I think we should get back on the interstate," he said, "I don't care if it takes longer."

"You're not scared, are you?" I looked over at him.

"No," he replied a little too quickly.

"You are," I teased, "But you don't have to be," I tried to placate him, "We're not going anywhere near Grove Hill."

"That's a relief," he sighed.

We drove on in silence for fifteen miles or so before Harrison started speaking again.

"You know they never caught the killer," he said.

Before I could reply, Harrison suddenly reached over and grabbed the steering wheel while shouting.

"Look out," he yelled.

I had looked over at him when he started talking to me and missed the nail-studded boards that spanned the dark country road.

Harrison tried to yank the car to the side of the road so I would drive around them, but he wasn't fast enough.

I thumped over the boards and immediately heard all four of my tires pop.

I hit the brakes and brought the car to a screeching halt.

"I knew we shouldn't have come this way," Harrison whined.

I followed his gaze to where a large scruffy-looking man wearing dirty overalls stepped out into the middle of the road, blocking our path. In his hands was a chainsaw.

"Backup! Backup! Backup!" Harrison yelled, but I ignored him. Instead, I turned off the car and opened my door.

"What the hell are you doing?" he hissed.

"Calm down," I said, "I know him."

"You what?"

"Hey, Cousin Lee," I raised my hand in greeting, "I see you got my message."

He nodded, acknowledging my comment.

"Is that him?" he gestured at Harrison with the chainsaw.

"Yep," I smiled, "That's the guy who cheated on me."

When Harrison heard what I said, he threw open his car door and started running down the road away from us.

He didn't get very far before a middle-aged woman in a dirty sundress stepped out into his path and pointed a shotgun at him.

"Hi, Aunt Linda," I waved to the woman, "Make sure you don't kill him. Mom and Dad want to have a word with him first."

HEARTBREAKER

"What's the matter, dear?" my grandmother asked.

She'd come into the living room and found me pouting on the couch.

"I feel bad about breaking up with Arthur," I said.

"Why?" she asked, "I thought it wasn't working out between the two of you?"

"It wasn't," I sighed.

It really wasn't. Arthur and I wanted completely different things from life. The biggest thing being a family. He wanted kids, and I didn't.

He also wanted to stay in our small town and take over his father's business while I wanted to get the hell out of there.

We just weren't compatible, so I ended things before they got too serious.

"Then why are you sitting here moping?" She sat on the couch next to me and put her arm around my shoulders.

"Because I made him cry," I said.

"Oh, don't worry about that, honey. He'll get over it," my grandmother explained. "Everyone gets their heart broken at some point. He should be grateful it was you who did it and not some-body else."

"Why do you say that?" I thought that was an odd thing to say.

"Because I know a lot of women who wouldn't have been as nice about the breakup as you've been. Myself included." She placed a hand on her chest. "Out of all the women in the family, you have the kindest heart."

I appreciated the compliment, even though it didn't sound like one coming from her mouth.

"Do you remember the first heart you broke?" I asked.

"Of course I do," she smiled, "I was the same age as you, but I didn't just break his heart when I ended the relationship, I cut it out of his chest and ate it."

"What?" I was horrified by her comment.

"I'm just kidding, dear," she patted my hand before getting up and walking over to the curio shelf to retrieve a box.

"I didn't really eat it," she opened the box to reveal a shriv-eled-up heart nestled in a bed of red velvet. "But I did keep it."

She removed the heart from the box and held it up before her eyes.

"You'd be surprised how much power there is in a broken heart."

She put the heart back in the box and closed it.

"I could show you how to use that power to get anything and everything your heart desires." The friendly demeanor dropped from her face and was replaced by a look of disappointment, "But I don't think you have the stomach for it. As I said before, you're too kind."

I ignored her comment, "Does mom know you have that?" I asked instead, pointing at the box.

"Of course, your mother knows," my grandmother replied, the smile returning to her face. "She has one of her own at home. How else do you think she's managed to do so well for herself?"

GIRL SCOUT COOKIES

I walked up the unkept path to the dilapidated house at the end of our street. It was to be my last stop on my trip around the neighborhood selling Girl Scout cookies.

"I don't think Ms. Beldam is going to want to buy any cookies," my mom said, trying to stop me. "You know she doesn't like kids."

"Yes, she will," I replied. "She promised."

"I don't think she was being serious," my mom said, "I think she was just trying to get you to go away last time."

"Excuse me," a woman who was walking the other way interrupted my mom and I, "I'm looking for my son and I was wondering if you'd seen him." She handed a flyer to my mom that had a picture of a boy I recognized along with a description of the clothes he was last seen wearing.

My mom took the flyer and looked at it.

"I'm sorry, I haven't seen him," she said, handing the flyer back to her.

"What about you? Have you seen him?" the woman walked up to me and handed me the same flyer.

I shook my head and tried to give it back to her.

She held up a hand. "Keep it," she said, "In case you do happen to see him."

After the woman walked away, my mom looked at me and said, "That's why I don't want you out here doing this alone."

I'd originally wanted to walk around the neighborhood by myself, but being the overprotective parent my mom was, she wouldn't let me.

"Whatever," I mumbled, turning around to walk the rest of the way up to Ms. Beldam's porch, where I rang the doorbell.

"What do you want?" Ms. Beldam screeched before she opened the door, "Oh, it's you," she sneered once she opened it. "I thought I told you I wasn't going to buy any of your stupid cookies," she added.

"That's not what you said," I reminded her, "You said, '*the only way I'd buy any cookies from you is if you got that little bastard to stop egging my house*' and then you pointed at Robert who was playing with his friends," I reminded her.

"I suppose I did, didn't I," she agreed.

"And that's why I'm here to take your order," I said, handing her Robert's missing person flyer. "He won't ever egg your house again," I explained, "I made sure of it."

Ms. Beldam eyed me with a newfound respect.

"Come inside," she held the door open for me, "Let's see what kinds of cookies you got."

I turned around and gave my mom a thumbs-up.

She had a shocked look on her face as I went into Ms. Beldam's house to take her order.

BABY SHARK

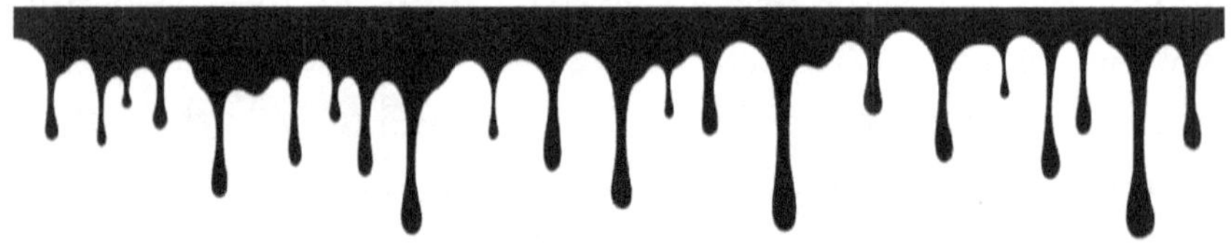

"**B**ABY SHARK! DOO DOO DOO DOO DOO DOO!"

Whoever was singing was doing it loud enough for the whole restaurant to hear.

When I turned around to see which table it was, I was mortified to see that it was one of mine.

I sighed in frustration. "Why do I always get the crazy people?"

I'd just taken their drink order and was in the process of filling it when the three of them, mother, father, and daughter, decided to break into song.

"It looks like your table is in a good mood," another waitress remarked.

"Lucky me," I quipped before picking up the drink tray and carrying it over to their table.

I'd hoped my arrival would prompt them to stop singing, but it didn't. They kept on belting out Baby Shark as I put their drinks on the table.

"Are you ready to order?" I asked.

The girl stopped singing and looked at me. "Not yet," she said.

I looked at the parents, waiting for them to say something, but they just ignored me and kept on singing.

"I'll come back in a few minutes," I whirled around and went to check on my other tables.

As I was doing that, my manager approached me and pulled me to the side.

"I've had several complaints about your table," he nodded toward them. "Can you please ask them to stop singing?"

Why can't you? I said in my head, even though I knew it was because he was a spineless coward who couldn't handle any kind of conflict from customers.

"Fine," I snapped and walked back over to the table.

I waited to see if the couple would acknowledge my presence, but they never did.

"I'm going to have to ask you to stop," I eventually said, trying to make myself heard over their singing, "It's disturbing the other diners."

"I don't care," the girl stopped singing to snap at me.

"Well, we do," I snapped back. "If you don't stop singing, I'm going to have to ask you to leave."

"I'll sing if I want to sing," she had a smug look on her face.

"Not here you won't."

"Oh yes I will," she folded her arms across her chest and narrowed her eyes.

Her parents continued to sing the entire time I exchanged words with their daughter.

"You need to leave." I pointed at the door.

"No," she shook her head.

I was about to turn around to go tell my manager to call the police, but I found myself unable to when the girl spoke to me inside my head.

Sit down! she commanded.

I didn't want to, but I was compelled to obey.

Once I was seated, the girl turned to me and smiled.

"Now start singing," she said out loud.

I joined her parents, singing Baby Shark as loud as I could.

When the manager finally came over, the girl slid a knife across the table to me.

"Make him go away," she said.

LIFE LIKE

I was on my way back to my bedroom when I heard a rustling sound coming from my sister, Erica's, room.

Thinking Erica was awake when she wasn't supposed to be, I crept over to her door and listened.

The rustling sound continued.

Wondering what she was doing, I eased the door open so I could see inside.

What I saw surprised me.

Erica wasn't the one making the noise. She couldn't, she was asleep in her bed. The noise was coming from one of the new dolls she'd gotten for her birthday.

It was lying on the floor, rolling around.

At first, I thought the doll was battery operated, and that Erica had forgotten to turn it off, but I quickly realized that was not the case when the seam on the doll's back split open and an ugly little impish creature climbed out of it.

I gasped.

It heard me.

It swung around and hissed before it started charging at me.

Afraid, I stumbled backward and hit the opposite wall of the hall.

I thought the creature was going to come and attack me, but that's not what it did. Instead, it shut the bedroom door.

"MOM! DAD!" I called for my parents as I rushed to the end of the hall.

"What's the matter, Kyle?" my dad sounded groggy and annoyed.

"There's a monster in Erica's room," I pointed.

It took his tired mind a moment to realize what I'd said.

"A what?"

"What's going on?" my mom asked behind him.

"Kyle says there's a monster in Erica's room," he replied to her.

"What was he doing in Erica's room?" she asked.

"I wasn't in her room," I clarified. "I heard something when I was walking down the hall, so I opened her door to see what it was and that's when I saw it."

Erica opened her door and stepped into the hall.

"Why is everyone awake?" she asked.

"There's a monster in your room," I answered.

"No there's not," my dad pushed past me, "Come on," he picked Erica up and carried her back into her room, "Let's get you back to bed."

"There is," I insisted, following him into the room. "It came out of this doll." I picked it up, expecting to find the split seam where the monster had crawled out of, but there wasn't one.

The doll felt like a normal doll stuffed with plush.

"Go to bed," my dad said.

"But," I tried to protest.

"No buts," he said, "Bed! Now!"

Frustrated, I went back to my room and climbed into bed, where I lay for an hour before finally passing out.

The feeling of something tapping on my forehead woke me a short time later.

When I opened my eyes, I was shocked to see one of my teddy bears standing on my chest with a knife in its hand.

Before I could cry out for help, it lifted its free hand and said, "Shh."

SISTERS

"What do you mean you've been sleeping with my boyfriend?" I snapped.

"Was sleeping with him," my sister, Alice, corrected me, "I broke it off with him months ago."

"Why are you telling me this now?"

"Because I want to get married with a clear conscience," was her reply.

"Does that mean you told Brad?" That was her fiancé's name.

"No, I haven't," she shook her head, "And I'm not going to."

Hearing her reply confirmed my suspicions that she was lying about her motivation for telling me.

"You're not trying to clear your conscience," I pointed an accusing finger at her, "You just don't want me to be a part of the wedding."

"That's not it," she said unconvincingly.

"Whatever," I stormed out of her apartment, slamming the door behind me.

The first thing I did after I left was confront my boyfriend.

He tried to lie about the affair at first, but changed his story once I told him that my sister had already confessed.

He begged for forgiveness and tried to pin the blame on Alice, saying she was the one who initiated things, but I didn't care.

It takes two to tango, was the last thing I said to him.

The next week was a series of emotional highs and lows for me until I decided that I wasn't going to let my sister get away with what she'd done.

After everything we'd been through over the years, she'd finally crossed a line, and I was going to make sure she paid for it.

Under the pretense of wanting to put things behind us, I reached out to Alice and invited her over to my apartment to make amends.

When she got there, I told her that it was over between my boyfriend and me and that we should celebrate.

She readily agreed and accepted the drug-laced drink I handed her.

"That was too easy," I said as I dragged her corpse into the bedroom where the body of my ex-boyfriend lay in a spreading pool of blood on the floor.

Before I positioned her body on the bed, I swapped the clothes I was wearing with the clothes she was wearing.

Since we were twins, nobody would be able to tell that it wasn't my body in the bed.

Now that the scene was set, I went back to Alice's apartment to enact the rest of my plan.

"How was your sister?" Brad asked when I walked through the door.

"I don't know," I replied, "She never answered the door."

"That's weird," he replied, "Why did she invite you over if she wasn't going to be there?"

"It is weird," I agreed, "Do you think I should call someone to check on her?" I asked.

"Nah," he shook his head, "You know how crazy she is. It's probably best to just forget about her."

"Yeah," I smiled, "You're probably right."

SOUVENIR PHOTO

"That's disgusting," my wife, Jennifer, pointed at the display.

It depicted a tribe of people eating one of their own.

According to the description, the tribe depicted believed that consuming the dead was a sign of love and respect.

The display was part of the *Funerals Around the World* exhibit at the Funeral Museum we'd decided to visit after finding the brochure for it in the lobby of our hotel.

"I don't know," I eyed her, "You look pretty tasty. I might have to take a bite out of you when you die."

"Ugh," she groaned, "Why do you have to be so gross?"

"I thought that's why you married me?"

"I married you for your money," Jennifer smiled. "If you weren't rich, your gross ass would be single."

I clutched my chest, feigning that she'd mortally wounded me with her comment.

"That would be ironic," she said.

"What would?"

"You dying in a funeral museum."

"That would be weird," I agreed.

"Come on," Jennifer started walking towards the next exhibit. "Let's keep moving."

We walked through the remaining exhibits, talking about the various gruesome funeral rites on display until we reached the gift shop.

"Do you want a souvenir?" I gestured at the shelves of funeral-themed merchandise laid out before us.

"I don't think so."

"Can I interest you in a personalized photo?" the pale man behind the counter asked.

He was clearly dressed up to look like a funeral director.

I walked up to the counter and looked at the two macabre photos he had lying on the counter, one of me, and one of my wife.

The photos showed a close-up of each of us lying in a coffin.

"I don't look that old, do I?" Jennifer asked.

In the photo, she looked about 15—20 years older than she did now. So did I.

"How did you make these?" I asked.

"We have special cameras throughout the facility," the man replied.

"It looks like they used some kind of filter," Jennifer said, "Like they do on TikTok."

"How much are they?"

"They're free with admission," he slid the photos over to me.

"Cool, thanks." I picked them up and started walking away.

"Why would you want those?" Jennifer sneered, "They're so morbid."

I ignored her and examined the photos. "Look, they have dates on the back," I pointed. "I wonder what they're for."

The dates, which were 17 years in the future, were the same on each photo.

When I turned around to ask the man about them, he was gone. Standing in his place was a young woman.

"Excuse me," I said, "Do you know what these dates mean?" I pointed to the backs of the photos.

"No," she replied. "Where did you get them?"

"That other guy who works here gave them to us," I said.

"What guy?" she asked.

I described him.

"Nobody like that works here," she replied, "And we don't give out morbid death photos like that."

ROOM 322

"I've been waiting for towels for over an hour," Mrs. Schmidt complained.

"I'm sorry," I apologized, "I'll go get you some."

I stepped away from the desk and into the backroom where we kept some extra supplies.

"Here you go," I set a stack of towels on the counter, "Is there anything else I can help you with?"

"Actually, there is," she said. "You can upgrade my room like you did for that couple."

"I'm sorry, but I can't do that."

"Why not?" she raised her voice, "You did it for them." She swept her arm toward the couple who were stepping onto the elevator.

"That wasn't my decision," I explained, "My manager upgraded them because the room they were staying in had a leak."

"My room has a leak too," Mrs. Schmidt quickly blurted out, which I knew was a lie.

"I can have maintenance come to your room," I countered.

"I don't want maintenance to come to my room," she snapped, "I want a new room."

"I can't just give you a new room."

"What seems to be the problem?" My manager, Brenda, who was watching the exchange between Mrs. Schmidt and me on the cameras, stepped out of her office.

"Mrs. Schmidt would like us to upgrade her room," I explained.

"Is there something wrong with the room you have now?" she asked Mrs. Schmidt.

"The bathtub leaks," she said, "And there is a weird smell in the room," she added.

"I'm sorry to hear that," Brenda replied, "Of course we'll upgrade you."

"Put her in room 322," Brenda said to me.

"Are you sure?" I asked.

"I'm positive," Brenda smiled.

"Okay," I prepared a new keycard and handed it to Mrs. Schmidt, who snatched it out of my hand with a smug look on her face.

"Let us know if we can be of any further help," Brenda said sarcastically as Mrs. Schmidt turned around and walked back towards the elevator.

———

10 minutes later, Mrs. Schmidt called the front desk from room 322.

"I think you put me in the wrong room," she said.

"Why do you think that?" I replied.

"There's somebody else's suitcase sitting on the bed."

"Really," I pretended I didn't know why the suitcase was there, "There shouldn't be."

"Well, there is," she sounded annoyed.

"It might've been left behind," I said, "Can you do me a favor and open the suitcase and see if you can find any kind of identification inside?"

"You want me to open it?"

"Yes, please."

"Okay," I heard her unzip the bag.

As soon as it was open, the sound of rushing air was all I could hear. This was followed by a scream as Mrs. Schmidt was sucked into the void that was inside the suitcase.

I waited until the sound receded before I hung up and called housekeeping.

"Can you please send someone up to clean room 322," I said, "The guest that was staying there has decided to check out early."

WICKED

"I know you don't want to stay here any longer than you have to," Grandma Edna said, "So, I'll make a deal with you. You can go home as soon as you finish this book." She held up a tattered and worn copy of *The Wizard of Oz*.

"I've already read that," Melissa said, "And seen the movie."

"I can assure you that you haven't read this version of the story," Grandma Edna insisted as she set the book down on the nightstand.

"Fine... whatever, just leave me alone," Melissa snapped.

"I meant what I said," Grandma Edna smiled. "Read the book and you get to go home." She started to close the bedroom but stopped, "And don't try to lie about it. I'll know if you've read it or not." When she was done talking, she shut the door.

Melissa was taken to her grandmother's house after she'd repeatedly gotten into trouble at school.

"Make her read the book," Melissa's mother had said to Grandma Edna when she'd dropped her daughter off.

The book she was referring to was no ordinary book. It was a magical book capable of transporting the reader into a fantasy world where they became the hero of the story while learning several valuable life lessons about courage, friendship, and responsibility.

Grandma Edna had used the book on all her children, and they became better people because of it. That's why she wasn't surprised when Melissa and her mother showed up.

After shutting the bedroom door, Grandma Edna stood in the hall for several minutes, waiting to see if Melissa would read the book. When she heard the familiar whooshing sound of the book's magic, she knew she had.

Just to make sure, she peeked into the room. When she saw that her granddaughter was gone, she smiled.

Several hours later, Grandma Edna heard the whooshing noise again. This time she knew it was the sound of the book returning Melissa to the bedroom.

"Have you..." Grandma Edna was about to ask Melissa if she'd learned her lesson, but the question died on her lips.

All she could do was stare at her granddaughter and the transformation she'd undergone.

Melissa was no longer wearing the jeans and a t-shirt she'd arrived in. She was now in a black dress that covered her legs and arms. On her head was a pointy black hat while a brain made from woven straw, a clockwork heart, and a bloody lion's tail hung from the belt around her waist. On her feet were two ruby slippers.

"There's no place like home," Melissa flashed a wicked smile.

"What have you done?" Grandma Edna gasped.

"I've become the me I was always meant to be," Melissa smiled. "Now, call my mother and tell her to come and pick me up. She and I need to have a long overdue chat."

DIRTY BOY

"What are you doing out here, retard?" Blaine said.

He and Carson were walking through the neighborhood when they came upon Quinn in one of the vacant lots.

"Nothing," Quinn replied softly, "Just playing."

Quinn was an autistic boy in the same grade as Blaine and Carson, but he wasn't in the same class as them. Like many autistic kids, Quinn was extremely sensitive to a variety of sensory stimuli, making it difficult for him to be with his peers. Because of that, he was placed in a special class. A class that Blaine assumed was for stupid kids.

"What's that supposed to be?" Blaine pointed at the shaped mound of dirt Quinn was kneeling next to.

"Nothing." Quinn stood up and backed away from his creation.

"It looks like a person," Carson said.

"You're right, it does," Blaine agreed.

It was a person. Quinn had created it to be his imaginary friend.

Feeling uncomfortable around the two boys, Quinn turned and started walking back towards his house. Normally his mother would be sitting on the porch watching him, but she had gone inside to put Quinn's sister down for her nap.

"Where do you think you're going?" Blaine quickly moved to block Quinn's path.

Quinn ignored Blaine's question and tried to walk around him.

"I didn't say you could leave." Blaine pushed Quinn.

Quinn looked towards his house, hoping his mother would come out and make the boys leave, but she was nowhere in sight.

"Your mama's not here to save you this time," Blaine taunted, pushing Quinn again, making him stumble backward into Carson.

Annoyed by the collision, Carson pushed Quinn away, causing the autistic boy to fall onto the ground, where he hit his mouth on a rock.

Blood gushed from a cut on Quinn's lip. He started crying immediately.

"What are you boys doing?" Quinn's mother yelled. She'd come back onto the porch and saw Blaine and Carson standing over her son.

The two boys took off running.

Quinn's mother rushed over to the vacant lot.

"I'm sorry honey," she apologized as she helped him to his feet and started leading him back to the house.

Blood and tears flowed freely down Quinn's face, dropping onto the dirt mound that was shaped like a person. When he looked down, he noticed that the drops had made a pattern on the part of the mound that was meant to be the head.

It looks like two eyes and a mouth. The thought flashed quickly through his mind and then was forgotten.

Later that night, after Quinn had gone to sleep, the boy made of dirt began to stir and free himself from the ground. Once he was on his feet, he turned and looked at Quinn's house.

"Friend," he said. His voice sounded like rocks grating against each other.

Then he turned and faced the neighborhood, setting his eyes upon Blaine's house.

"Not friend," he growled as he left the vacant lot.

MARIANNE

"Get your ass in there," The taller of the two men who had kidnapped me violently shoved me into the dimly lit bathroom and locked the door.

"Let me out," I screamed while banging on the door.

In an effort to get home and not be late, I'd decided to take a shortcut down an alley that ran behind some houses on the edge of my neighborhood.

I'd taken that shortcut dozens of times and never thought I'd ever be in any kind of danger. Boy, was I wrong.

I banged on the door for about 5 minutes before I gave up and decided to look around and see if there was anything I could use to pry the door open or defend myself.

There wasn't anything.

The bathroom was in a state of disrepair. The area where the toilet was supposed to be was empty. All that remained was a hole in the ground. The sink was missing its fixtures and the cabinet below it was missing its doors.

The only other things in the bathroom were a dirty mirror hanging on the wall and a single light bulb in the ceiling.

I might be able to use that, I thought as I looked at my grime-stained reflection in the mirror.

I could break it and use one of the shards as a knife.

As I stared into the mirror, I noticed that someone had etched the name Marianne into the bottom corner of it.

Marianne was the name of a girl who'd gone missing in our neighborhood over a year ago. I didn't think it was a coincidence that her name was in that bathroom.

Seeing it made me realize the seriousness of my situation. Marianne hadn't left that house alive, and I wasn't going to either unless I did something about it.

Knowing that I didn't have much time, I took off one of my socks and wrapped it around my hand so I wouldn't cut myself when I broke the mirror. Then I pulled my arm back and got ready to swing. But the swing never happened.

As I stared at the mirror, preparing to break it, an image of a blood-covered girl appeared. A girl I recognized.

"Marianne?" I gasped.

The image of her appeared for only a moment, but it was long enough for me to see that she was shaking her head, warning me not to break the mirror.

But why? Why would she try to stop me? *Unless...*

It was a stupid idea, but I figured it was worth a try.

I looked into the mirror and said, "Bloody Mary."

The light in the ceiling flickered.

"Bloody Mary," I repeated.

The walls of the bathroom started to tremble.

I smiled.

Marianne was about to have her revenge, and those guys were never going to know what hit them.

"Bloody Mary," I said a final time.

The bathroom light went out, and the screams began.

GARDEN PARTY

“Hi, Ms. Green,” I said as she opened the door, “I’m Jasmine.”

“Hello, Jasmine,” Ms. Green replied, “I hope you had no trouble finding the place. And please call me Flora.”

“It was no trouble,” I lied.

Getting to her house was a bit stressful. The map app I was using said the address didn’t exist and then I lost cell signal on the way and would’ve gotten lost if it weren’t for the detailed directions Ms. Green had given me.

“Come inside,” She stepped aside so I could enter the house.

“Oh my god,” I gasped upon seeing the interior of her home.

There were flowering plants everywhere. It felt like I had walked into an exotic garden.

“Do you like it?”

“It’s beautiful,” I replied.

Ms. Green smiled, “With a name like Jasmine, I figured you would.”

“Is this the one you chose?” a deep voice asked from behind me.

I turned around and was shocked to see a tall, muscular man wearing the armor of a centurion.

"She's a bit small, don't you think?" he added.

"Don't mind, Mars," Ms. Green said, "He's always trying to start trouble. Come, let's get you situated." She placed her arm around my shoulders and led me through the house to the back-yard.

"Is this a costume party?" I asked upon seeing all the people dressed in various Roman costumes milling about.

Ms. Green laughed.

"I'm afraid not," she smiled, "The people before you are my fellow gods and goddesses. We come together at this time every year to celebrate the Floralia."

"Oh," was all I could think to say while in my head I thought: *I've accepted a job from a bunch of crazy people.*

"That's Neptune, god of the sea" she pointed at a shirtless man with bronze skin, "And that's Diana, goddess of the hunt," she pointed at a woman with a bow slung across her back, "And that's..." she kept pointing out people introducing them before ending with, "And you've already met Mars," she gestured at the armored man.

"I'm sorry," I apologized, "But I don't think I'm the right person for this job." I started backing away towards the house.

"Of course you are, dear," Ms. Green said to me, "You wouldn't have made it here if you weren't."

"I'm gonna go."

I quickly walked through the house, intending to leave. But I only made it to the front porch.

"Where the hell is my car?" It was not where I parked it.

"A sacrifice must be made," Ms. Green said after joining me on the front porch, "Otherwise the flowers will not bloom in the spring and the Earth will be subject to another 12 weeks of winter."

"You're nuts," I snapped and then started walking toward the road.

"If you come willingly, I promise to make it painless."

"Fuck you!" I started running.

"Oh, Diana!" Ms. Green called out, "It looks like you're going to get to go on a hunt after all!"

ANNA

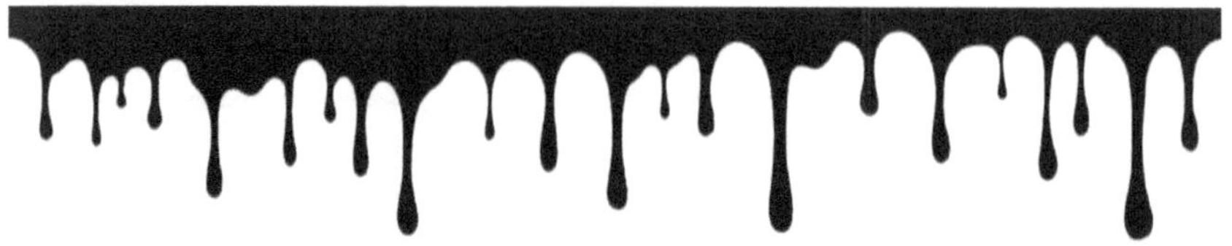

"**W**hat is your sister doing?" I asked.

My girlfriend, Hailee, followed my gaze to where her sister was squatting at the edge of the playground looking at something on the ground.

"Oh shit," Hailee jumped up from the bench and raced over her sister.

I quickly followed behind, wondering what all the fuss was about.

"Don't even think about touching that, Anna," Hailee snapped.

"I wasn't going to," Anna replied, "I was just looking at it."

Lying on the ground between Anna's feet was a dead squirrel.

"Come on," Hailee reached down and pulled Anna to her feet, "We're leaving."

"But we just got here," Anna pouted while trying to pull away from her sister's grasp.

"What's going on?" I asked.

"We have to leave," Hailee said, dragging her sister along the sidewalk toward the street.

"Is it because of the squirrel?" I looked over at the carcass of the small rodent, wondering what the big deal was. "I can get rid of it," I offered.

Hailee ignored me and kept walking.

"Why do you have to leave?" I asked, after catching up with them.

"You wouldn't understand," Hailee replied.

"Try me," I said, but she didn't get a chance to respond.

Before she could open her mouth, Anna lifted her foot and brought it down as hard as she could on Hailee's toes.

Then she spat in her face and yelled, "I hate you."

When Hailee reflexively let go of Anna to wipe the spit off her face, Anna took off running across the street.

"Get back here!" Hailee said as she started running after her sister.

She was so focused on catching Anna that she didn't see the car coming until it was too late.

There was nothing the driver could do to prevent hitting Hailee.

I watched in horror as my girlfriend's body flew through the air and landed on the ground twenty feet away.

"Call 911!" I yelled repeatedly as I rushed over to where her motionless body lay on the ground.

When I saw the odd way her neck was bent, I knew she was dead.

"Hailee?" I heard Anna say behind me.

Not wanting her to see her sister's body, I quickly turned around and tried to shield her, but she darted around me and ran over to her sister's body.

"She's gone." I tried to gently steer her away, but she shrugged me off and dropped to her knees next to Hailee.

Seeing her like that broke my heart, at least it did until I saw what she did next.

"Please don't be dead," Anna sobbed while reaching out and placing her hands on her sister's chest.

I started crying too, but I stopped when I saw one of Hailee's arms twitch. A second later, the other arm twitched. Then she sat up.

When she did, she had to support her head with both hands to keep it upright and looking forward.

"What have you done?" Hailee glared at Anna.

THE COVER UP

My partner, Officer Blake, looked down at the body of the homeless man who was lying on the ground in the alley behind the convenience store.

"Oh shit," he nudged the body with his shoe, "I think he's dead."

"Well, you did hit him pretty hard," I gestured at the bloody gash on top of the man's head.

"He was coming at me," Blake said. "What was I supposed to do?"

The homeless man wasn't coming at him by any stretch of the imagination. He was clearly drunk and stumbled into Blake. Blake, being the germophobe that he is, overreacted by pushing the guy away and hitting him with his baton.

I leaned down and checked the man's pulse just to be sure.

"Yep, he's dead," I confirmed.

"Shit," Blake hissed, "They're going to fire me for this." He ran a hand through his hair as he thought about the implications of what he had done.

He was exaggerating. They wouldn't fire him. Worst-case scenario, he'd be suspended without pay for a month.

"Do you want to call it in, or do you want me to?" I offered.

"I'll do it," he replied, "But first we need to get our stories straight."

"Whatever you say, man," I said, letting him know I was on his side, "I'll follow your lead. This doesn't look good for me either." I gestured at the body.

"That's right," he quickly latched onto the idea of us both being culpable.

Blake paced back and forth for a moment, trying to come up with a story that would fit the scene.

"Here's what we're going to say," he stopped pacing and came over to stand beside me, "We're going to say he fled when we arrived and attacked me with that broken beer bottle when I came around the corner. I had no choice but to defend myself."

The man hadn't fled. We'd found him sitting on the ground behind the convenience store where he was drinking the bottle of malt liquor he'd stolen.

"That sounds good to me," I said.

Given that the victim was homeless, the detectives who arrived to question us accepted our version of events and were content to close the case.

When our shift ended, Blake stopped me on my way out of the station.

"Want to grab a few beers?" he asked.

"Sorry, I wish I could," I apologized, "But I've got something I need to take care of."

"Another time then," he said.

"Another time," I agreed.

After I left the station, I drove to the hospital where I used my badge to gain access to the morgue. Once inside the autopsy suite, I found the drawer that held the body of the homeless man and pulled it out.

"Rise and shine," I said, opening the dead man's mouth and sprinkling voodoo powder into it. "You've got unfinished business with Officer Blake."

THE POET

"What do you think is in here?" my wife, Vicky, held up a small plastic case.

"Knowing my mom, it's probably recipes," I replied.

The two of us were cleaning out my mother's house after she'd passed away.

Vicky opened the box, pulled out the first card, and looked at it.

"This isn't a recipe," she said. "It's poetry."

She showed me the card. Handwritten on it in calligraphy were two lines of poetry:

A seed will not always bloom,
but it will grow nonetheless.

"Do you recognize it?" I asked.

Vicky was more knowledgeable about that sort of thing than I was.

"I don't think your mom copied this," she replied, "I think she wrote it herself. Along with the rest of these." She looked down at the box and ran her fingers along the cards.

"Huh," I said, honestly surprised by the discovery, "My mom was a poet and I didn't even know it."

Vicky groaned, "Talent is clearly not genetic," she smirked, "Speaking of which, shouldn't you have gotten the results of your DNA test back by now?"

She was referring to the DNA test I'd sent to Ancestry.com in the hopes of finding a familial tie that would help me figure out who my father was.

My mother would never tell me who he was.

"I was supposed to get them last week," I replied, "If I don't get them by the end of this week, I'm going to email them."

"Good idea," My wife agreed.

She put the box of poetry cards with the rest of the stuff we were kept and then went back to helping me sort through my mother's things.

Three days later, I was shocked when Vicky came into the living room and told me there were two FBI agents at the door asking for me.

"Are you Kyle Chapman?" the taller of the two asked.

"I am."

"I'm Agent Grey and this is Agent Harris," he introduced himself and his partner while flashing his badge. "Can we talk to you for a moment?"

"What about?"

He reached into the pocket of his suit, withdrew a folded-up piece of paper, and handed it to me. When I looked at it, I saw that it was the results of a DNA test.

"We have reason to believe you are the missing son of a murder victim from the late 70s," the agent explained.

"Murder victim?" I was shocked to hear that.

The agent nodded. "He was killed by a serial killer the press was calling The Poet."

"The Poet?" Still in shock at what I'd been told, I just parroted what he said.

"He was called that because he would leave these hand-written poetry cards on the victim."

The agent showed me a poetry card that looked exactly like the ones Vicky and I had found at my mother's house.

"We're hoping you might be able to tell us who he is."

"Who she is," I corrected him.

DR. MARKHAM

I made it to the therapist's office right as the doctor was unlocking the door.

"Excuse me," I said, "Are you Dr. Markham?"

Startled, the doctor jumped and whirled around to face me.

"Oh my God," she had a hand on her chest, "You scared the crap out of me."

"Sorry," I apologized.

"How can I help you?" the doctor asked.

"I was wondering if I could talk to you for a moment," as I spoke, I couldn't keep my eyes from tearing up, "About my husband."

Dr. Markham stared at me, taking note of the bruises on my arms and neck.

"Yeah," she replied, "Come inside."

She opened the door and then led me into an inner office where she gestured at a chair in front of a large desk and said, "Have a seat."

Dr. Markham waited until I was seated before seating herself behind the desk.

"Here." She held out a box of tissues. After I took one and dried my eyes, she said, "Now tell me about your husband."

Over the next thirty minutes, I told her about all of the abuse I'd suffered at my husband's hands and how he manipulated all of the people who were supposed to help me, making them believe whatever story he concocted to explain my injuries.

When I was done speaking, Dr. Markham leaned forward.

"You're not alone," she said. "Thousands of women go through the same thing every day."

"How do they survive?"

"Most of them don't," she frowned, "But." She got up, came around the desk, and sat on the edge of it, "That's because they didn't know help was available."

"What kind of help?"

"My kind of help," she smiled and gestured at herself.

Before I could respond, she started talking again.

"Here's what I need you to do," she went back to the other side of the desk and searched through the drawers until she found the form she was looking for, "I need you to fill this out and then go stay with a friend or coworker. Someone your husband doesn't know. I'll take care of everything else."

I tried to ask her to explain further, but she wouldn't. She just had me fill out the form and then ushered me out of her office.

Later that day, I did as she said, choosing to stay with a young woman I worked with who had been sympathetic to my problems. While the two of us were eating dinner, I got a call from the police.

They told me my husband was dead. Victim of a botched burglary.

The next day, after the morgue returned my husband's personal effects, I found Dr. Markham's business card tucked into the pocket of his jeans.

Confused, I went to the doctor's office the next day where I encountered a woman I didn't recognize. She was overseeing the changing of the office locks.

"Do you know where Dr. Markham is?" I asked her.

"I'm Dr. Markham," she replied.

LOCKDOWN

T he red light on the ceiling of the lab started flashing when the alarm went off.

"That can't be good," I said.

"It's not." Sherri walked over to the computer to see if she could figure out what was going on.

The two of us were in the lab waiting for our teacher to show up so we could use the particle accelerator to run our experiment when the alarm started.

"The particle accelerator is overheating." Sherri pointed at the monitor that was flashing a warning message.

"What do you mean it's overheating?" I said, "It's not supposed to be running."

"Well, it is," Sherri pointed.

"Can you turn it off?"

Sherri began frantically typing on the keyboard before turning to me with a worried look on her face.

"It's not responding," she said.

"Keep trying," I rushed over to the lab door. "I'm going to see if I can find someone to help us."

I pushed against the door, expecting it to swing open but it remained shut. Thinking I did something wrong, I pushed again but it still wouldn't open.

"We're locked in," I jiggled the door handle.

"What do you mean we're locked in?" Sherri asked, "That door locks from this side. It's impossible to get locked in."

"Tell that to the door," I snapped.

"This is really bad," Sherri fretted, "We can't be in here if the accelerator overloads."

"What'll happen if it overloads?"

"I have no idea," she said, "I can't see the parameters it's running under. All I know for sure is it won't be good."

"Isn't there a failsafe?" I recalled the teacher mentioning something about that when he gave us a tour of the lab earlier in the semester.

"There is," Sherri confirmed. "But it's in there with the accelerator."

"Well, what are we waiting for? Let's get in there and shut it down." I crossed the lab and approached the door that led to the accelerator room.

"Wait," Sherri yelled as I was about to touch the door handle, "Check it first," she instructed. "According to this," she gestured at the monitor, "It's 110 degrees in there."

I tapped the handle, testing the temperature. It felt a little warm but not hot.

"Come on," I yanked open the door, "We need to shut it down before it gets any hotter."

"Where is the failsafe?" I asked.

"Over there," Sherri pointed at a big red button on the wall.

I ran across the room and slapped the button with my open hand.

The accelerator immediately shut down, as did the alarm.

Suddenly, the door that was locked swung open. Standing on the other side of it was our teacher.

"Hurry up and get out of there before the accelerator starts another time loop," he yelled from the doorway. "Your bodies can't handle much more of this."

Before we could comprehend what he was saying, everything started moving in reverse and we found ourselves back at the beginning of our ordeal.

TEACHER

"Alright, Angela," the principal called me into his office, "What's this big problem that couldn't wait until after lunch?"

I stepped into his office and took a seat in front of the desk, waiting until he was also seated before I said anything.

"Do you believe in demons, Principal Roberts?" I asked.

"In what?" he looked at me like I was crazy.

"Demons," I repeated.

He stared at me for a moment, choosing how best to respond to my question before he spoke.

"Do you believe in demons?" he asked, clearly wondering if I had lost my mind.

"I do," I insisted, "And I can prove they exist."

"Is that right?" he sounded patronizing.

"I can," I huffed, "Call Ms. Jones in here and I'll prove it to you."

Ms. Jones was my 4th-period English teacher. Ever since the start of the semester, she'd been acting weird. Doing things like muttering to herself in weird languages, drawing strange shapes on the papers she graded, and dressing a bit more provocatively than I thought appropriate for a teacher.

At first, I just thought she might be going through a midlife crisis or something. But I realized that wasn't the case when I saw her eyes become solid black.

It happened two days ago when Carlton, one of the school's star football players, flicked a paper football across the room where it struck Ms. Jones in the back.

She whirled around and strode straight up to Carlton's desk, lifting him out of his chair by his shirt. When she did, I happened to look at her face and that's when I saw her black eyes.

They only stayed black for a moment, but that was enough for me to realize there was something seriously wrong with Ms. Jones.

That night, I went home and researched black eyes and there was only one explanation I could find: Demonic possession.

I related all this to Principal Roberts. When I was done, he leaned forward and said, "Do you know how crazy that sounds?"

"Just call her in here." I reached into my pocket, withdrew the bottle of holy water I'd filled at the church, and set it on the desk, "I can prove she's a demon."

"I wouldn't normally indulge a student like this," Principal Roberts explained, "But I will make an exception, just to put your mind at ease."

When he was done speaking, he called Ms. Jones to the office.

"You wanted to see me?" Ms. Jones said after she'd entered the office.

"I didn't," he replied, "Angela did." He pointed at me.

I reached out to grab the bottle of holy water, but accidentally knocked it over instead. It splashed against Principal Robert's hand, making his skin burn.

His eyes turned black.

"That was unfortunate," he smiled.

I jumped up and tried to flee, but I didn't get very far. Half of the faculty was standing just outside the office, blocking my path.

They all had black eyes.

THE CONDUCTOR

The sound of a train whistle startled little Billy awake.

He sat up in bed and looked around, wondering if the sound had come from a dream.

Outside, the train whistled again.

Billy threw off the covers, climbed out of bed, and walked over to the window. When he pulled the curtains aside, he was surprised to see a steam locomotive in his backyard.

The conductor of the train leaned out of the locomotive and waved at Billy before motioning for him to open the window.

Billy, who was a huge fan of trains, couldn't believe his luck. He'd always wanted to ride in the engine of a train and now there was one parked behind his house.

He pushed open the window and leaned out.

"Excuse me, young man," the conductor called out, "My fireman quit on me and now I'm stuck here in what I presume to be your backyard." He gestured at the yard around him. "If it's not too much bother, do you think you could help me get the engine going again?"

"How?" Billy asked, "I'm too small to shovel coal."

He knew enough about trains to know that the fireman's job was to shovel coal into the firebox to keep the engine running.

"Right you are," the conductor agreed. "That's why you're going to be the engineer," he pointed at Billy, "And I'm going to be the fireman." He pointed at himself.

"But I don't know how to drive the train?" Billy said.

He knew that the engineer's job was to control all the essential functions of the train, like the speed.

"It's actually quite easy," the conductor said, "Come on down and I can show you everything you need to know."

"I don't know." Billy wasn't sure it was a good idea.

"I promise you that it's okay," the conductor insisted, "In fact, I guarantee that your parents would want you to help me."

"You know my parents?" Billy was surprised to hear that.

"I do," the conductor smiled, "Mr. and Mrs. Willoughby are the best parents a boy like you could ask for. So, what do you say, are you in or out?"

Billy thought about it for a while.

"Time's a ticking, Billy. I have a schedule to keep. If you're not coming, I need to find somebody else to help me run the train," the conductor said.

"I'm in," Billy declared. He knew he was never going to get another chance like this.

As he climbed out of his bedroom window, he never once looked back at his bed. If he had, he would've seen his body lying motionless under the covers.

"What's your name?" Billy asked the conductor as he climbed aboard the train, "I'm Billy," he introduced himself.

"I've had many names over the years," the conductor replied, "But these days most people just call me Death."

A LIFETIME OF PUZZLES

"D id he fall or was he pushed?" Detective Bryan asked.

"Why are you asking me?" the coroner looked up at the detective from where she was squatting next to the body of a man who appeared to be in his late 50s or early 60s, "Isn't it your job to figure that out?"

"I thought you might have an opinion on the matter," the detective said.

"Well, I don't," the coroner replied, "All I can tell you is that his injuries are consistent with a tumble down the stairs," she gestured behind them at the flight of steps leading to the second floor, "I won't be able to tell you anything else until I get him on the table and open him up."

"Does this belong to the deceased?" Detective Bryan leaned over and picked up a book that was lying partly under an accent table in the foyer.

The coroner shrugged and opened her mouth to say something, but the detective stopped her with an outstretched hand.

"I know, I know," he said. "It's my job to figure it out."

Detective Bryan carried the book outside to where the deceased's teenage grandchildren were waiting. They were the ones who'd found the body when they'd arrived home from school.

"Did this belong to your grandfather?" He held the book up.

The boy nodded.

"He always carried that around with him," the girl said. "He wouldn't let anyone else touch it. I tried to sneak a peek at it years ago, but he caught me and chewed me out. I haven't tried to look at it since."

Detective Bryan turned the book around so he could examine it better.

A Lifetime of Puzzles. He read the title to himself.

"What's so special about it?"

Neither of the grandkids could answer that question.

Curious, Detective Bryan opened the book to the first page and was shocked by what he read.

A Lifetime of Puzzles Welcomes Jim Bryan to the Game.

What the hell is my name doing in this book?

He turned the page and continued reading.

The rules of the game are simple. Every Monday you will be given a new puzzle to solve. For every puzzle you solve, your life is guaranteed until the next puzzle is revealed. However, if you fail to solve the given puzzle before the next one is revealed, your life is forfeit.

The current record holder is Jensen Porter, who guaranteed his life for 1,508 weeks. Can you do better?

Jensen Porter was the name of the dead man on the floor inside the house

Turn the page for your first puzzle.

Detective Bryan turned the page.

Since this is your first week, we will start the game with something easy. All you have to do is solve the following anagram message. Hint: 4 words

Beneath the instructions were the following letters.

TGBLIDOUEROVCTYDEKEACN

You only get one guess. Make it count. Once you think you know the answer, write it in the space below.

SANTA'S LIST

Isabelle sat up in bed and listened. She was doing her best to fall asleep, but it was hard because she kept hearing the tinkling of bells out in the hall.

Stay in your room or Santa won't bring you any presents tonight. The words her mother had said to her when she tucked her in for the night echoed through her mind.

THUD!

Isabelle jumped when she heard the loud noise. It sounded like someone had dropped something really heavy in the room next door.

Or maybe someone fell down, Isabelle thought.

What if it was Santa? What if he got hurt and needs help?

She swung her legs out of bed and walked across the room to the door, placing her ear against it so she could listen.

She could still hear the tinkling of bells along with a new sound. The new sound was familiar, but it still took her a moment to realize what it was.

Something is being dragged across the carpet, she thought to herself.

She knew the sound because she often had to drag or push things down the hall that were too heavy for her, like the laundry basket when she was helping her mom put away the clean clothes.

Maybe it's Santa. Maybe he's crawling along the floor because he fell down and can't get back up.

The image of Santa pulling himself down the hall by his arms flashed through her mind.

I should go out there and check, she convinced herself, *Just to make sure he's okay.*

Isabelle cracked the door open far enough to peek her head out into the hall. When she saw the large figure in the red and white suit standing at the end of the hall with his back to her, she gasped.

It really is Santa!

At least she thought it was him until she realized that the figure's clothes were too dirty and disproportioned to be Santa Claus.

"You're not Santa," she said.

The figure in the Santa suit stopped and released the blanket-wrapped bundle he was dragging down the hall. When he did, a familiar-looking face appeared in the folds.

That's Thomas!

From the vacant look in her brother's eyes, she could tell he was dead.

The figure stopped and turned to face Isabelle, allowing her to see his monstrous features and the two curved horns sprouting from his head, dangling from which were several small bells.

"You're supposed to be asleep, little one," the monster in the Santa suit growled. "Best you go back to bed before I put you on the naughty list like your brother here." He shook the dead boy's ankle to emphasize his point.

Isabelle did as the monster instructed, shutting her door and returning to her bed with a huge smile on her face.

She was smiling because Santa had given her the one thing she'd wanted most for Christmas and that was for someone to come and take her brother away for good.

MORE CHILLS FROM VELOX BOOKS

MORE CHILLS FROM VELOX BOOKS

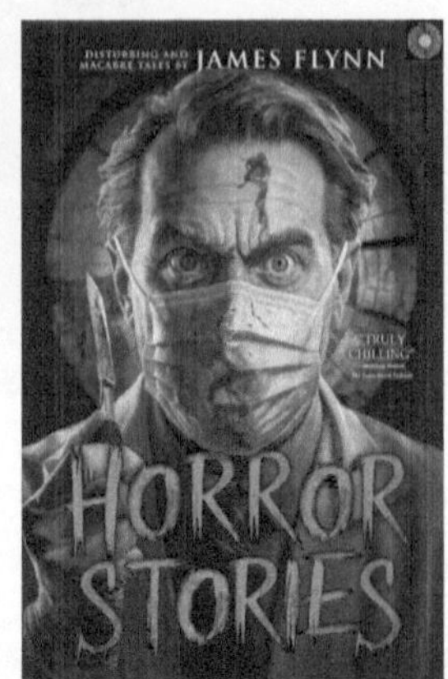

MORE CHILLS FROM VELOX BOOKS

9 781963 107500